Summer Road Trip

Golden

BY MARY VICTORIA JOHNSON

EPIC Escape

An Imprint of EPIC Press
abdopublishing.com

Golden
Summer Road Trip

Written by Mary Victoria Johnson

Published by EPIC Press™
PO Box 398166
Minneapolis, MN 55439

Printed in the United States of America.

Cover design by Christina Doffing
Images for cover art obtained from iStock
Edited by Rue Moran

LIBRARY OF CONGRESS CATALOGING-IN-PUBLICATION DATA
Names: Johnson, Mary Victoria, author.
Title: Golden/ by Mary Victoria Johnson
Description: Minneapolis, MN : EPIC Press, 2018 | Series: Summer road trip
Summary: Travelling to Canada to work as a tour guide was supposed to help Lewis figure out what to do with his life. But hitting British Columbia's Cariboo gold rush trail with a group of seniors goes from a chore to plain dangerous when a girl without a past joins. Soon, Lewis confronts a tangled mess of lies, accusations, and feelings he was totally unprepared for.
Identifiers: LCCN 2016962614 | ISBN 9781680767223 (lib. bdg.)
| ISBN 9781680767780 (ebook)
Subjects: LCSH: Adventure stories—Fiction. | Travel—Fiction.
| Tour guides (Persons)—Fiction. | Parks—British Columbia—Fiction
| Young adult fiction.
Classification: DDC [FIC]—dc23
LC record available at http://lccn.loc.gov/2016962614

Also for Mum

This one's for all the broccoli and cheese.

Chapter One

~~Dear~~ Hey Chrissy,

Thanks for writing! You must be the last person in the world to still send letters. Not that it's a bad thing. I have to say, it's harder to reply to a letter than an email, though.

Canada is great so far. It's so beautiful I'm surprised there aren't more people moving here. Aside from ~~crushing loneliness~~ the colder weather, I'm doing well. I've got my first tour starting next week. I'm kind of nervous, but at the same time, I'm dying to get started. There's only so much classroom time I can stand, considering it's summer.

Sorry I don't have more to say. ~~Nothing happens~~ It's

been super laid-back, aside from training. I'm sure I'll have more to say once I actually start working! Be nice to Mum, do your homework, etc. No boyfriends until I get back, okay?

~~Miss you~~

~~Love~~

Talk to you later!

Lewis

I reread the letter twice before sealing it in an envelope, making sure there weren't any errors for Chrissy to latch onto and berate me for. At fifteen, my sister was three years my junior, but that never stopped her from making sure I remembered we graduated together. She was starting university this coming September, majoring in biophysics. And I was here, earning less than what my rent cost, trying to figure out what I wanted to do with my life.

To balance out health and hunger, I decided to jog to a nearby pizza parlor for lunch after posting the letter. Then, triple checking I'd gotten the time right, I hopped on a bus to my boss's "office." The neighborhood was typical of North Vancouver, a mismatched collection of multimillion-dollar West Coast contemporary styles and more demure split-levels. Some were hidden behind massive hedges or wrought iron gates, others boasting wide open driveways to show off a collection of cars that were worth more than I'd ever touch in a lifetime. This was the land of new money, nestled in the space left between the cedar forests, mountains, and Pacific Ocean. It was also home to my employer.

I stood at the driveway of one of the neighborhood's more luxurious properties and pressed the buzzer on the gate.

"That you, Crake?"

"Uh, yes." *Should I have added "sir"? Or is that too formal? Is it possible to be too formal? I mean, I already have the job. It can't matter too much.*

The gates swung open. I realized then I was wearing my athletic gear. Excellent planning as per usual on my part.

The boss didn't open the door; his assistant did. Because yes, he was rich enough to have a live-in assistant.

"Lewis Crake," she smiled, pronouncing every syllable of my name. "Can I take your coat?"

"It's the middle of July," I pointed out. "I'm not wearing a coat."

"Tea, then?"

"Water would be fine."

"Ice?"

"Sure."

"Lemon?"

"Rachelle," my boss laughed from somewhere else in the house. "Let the poor boy go. Just come through to the main sitting area, Lewis."

The inside was all white marble and glass, and stunk of some artificial air freshener. It was the type of place I imagined was freezing in the winter.

David Swierenga lounged on a clear plastic chair, his bald forehead glinting in the sunlight. He could've been anywhere between thirty-five and sixty-five, depending on the angle, and I'd never found any evidence pointing to which end of the spectrum he likely belonged in. I knew from our previous meetings that he'd come from money, then doubled it as a real estate specialist, and now ran a multitude of small businesses just for fun. One such business was Golden Tours. That was why I was here.

"Enjoying the weather?" Swierenga asked, gesturing to the panoramic view. The skyscrapers of downtown Vancouver could just be seen through the trees of his neighbor's garden as well as the waters of Burrard Inlet, riddled with cargo ships, yachts, and sightseeing vessels.

"It's a different kind of heat than Australia," I said. "But yeah, I'm enjoying it."

"Just you wait until winter. Ever experience subzero?"

I shook my head. "I've never even seen snow."

Swierenga's grin widened. "Well, you just might have that pleasure sooner rather than later. Which leads us back to why you're here. You said you were willing to take our next tour group northward?"

I nodded, even now questioning how ready I actually was. I knew everything there was to know—from a tourism perspective at least—about half the municipalities in British Columbia. I'd taken numerous workshops and courses, I'd successfully completed a series of tests and interviews for Swierenga and, on occasion, Rachelle. But when it came to practical experience, I had nothing.

"Cariboo Gold Rush Trail," Swierenga said, laying out a map with a flourish. "Popular, nothing too complicated about the route. You aced this section on my test, if I remember correctly."

I nodded again. "I—"

"Now, I like you, Lewis. I don't usually hire foreigners, but you've got *it*. Charisma, charm, whatever kids are saying these days. And ultimately, that's all a tour guide has to have. So long as you make the paying guests happy, the rest is inconsequential." Swierenga leaned forward, and something in his stomach made a sloshing sound. "Good tour guide, good tour. Bad tour guide, bad tour. It's that simple. This company is my pet—that's why I'm talking to you directly, not through a manager—and the reputation of it rests on your shoulders. Nowadays, one dissatisfied customer can be enough to sink an entire ship. You get where I'm going?"

I'd had to bite my tongue to stop myself from pointing out that Golden Tours ran an ad in an Australian magazine, specifically targeting students who might want to work a summer abroad. I shook that thought away and grinned. "Of course. I'm honored you've put so much trust in me already."

Swierenga slid back in his chair, basking in the flattery. "Mostly old fogies on this route, anyway. They ask a lot of questions, but they don't get too caught up in the facts. They're suckers for bright young things like you, kid. Just make sure you keep an eye on health concerns and all that. Nobody's died on my watch, yet."

I managed to force a chuckle. "Nor on mine, yet."

"Well, all right." Swierenga stood up, offering me a hand to shake. "Give me or Rachelle a call if you have any issues. Oh, and before I forget, here's your advance. Do your job, and I'll see you in two weeks to hand over the rest."

My hand closed around the envelope. Rent, food, flights.

"Thank you," I said. "I won't let you down."

"Home" was a basement flat in a shabby complex in the more industrial part of outer Vancouver. Chrissy pointed out to me that I was paying more to live here than she was paying for tuition (pretending she didn't have a scholarship, of course), and Dad even calculated how nice a car I could've bought instead.

"You're wasting the best years of your life," he'd told me. "You're going to come home more broke than your Uncle Stewart, and with what to show for it?"

I remembered arguing that I was going to *Canada*, not some rinky-dink resort on a Queensland beach. He'd retorted by saying that if I wanted to travel, I should do it properly, not waste all my money boarding in one of the world's most expensive cities for a job in the tourism industry. But, me being me, I'd gone anyway. I was still trying to convince myself I'd done the right thing.

"Cole? You here, mate?" I called, hitting a light switch with my fist on the way in. It took a solid minute to turn on.

No answer. I was safe. My roommate commuted to a nearby college every day, which worked out well for both of us. We were rarely ever in together; I didn't even know his last name.

I ended up lying on my bed for far too long, staring at the ceiling in an effort to summon enough energy to do something, anything.

Dang, I miss home.

Eight weeks. That was all I had left. Swierenga had hinted at being able to get me another job over winter if I'd needed it, and as pathetic as it was, I wasn't sure if I could mentally last that long. Despite Vancouver being one of the most beautiful places I'd ever visited, I wasn't able to shake off the feeling of not belonging. That was why I needed to go on this tour. I needed to keep busy, I needed to get my head in the game and man up.

I was eighteen. Less than two months ago, I'd still been in high school, living off my mother's cooking and playing BS bingo instead of listening in business class. Now I was paying rent and cooking my own meager meals and, in a matter of days, would be responsible for thirty seniors.

My headache was what eventually drew me out of bed. I stumbled to the kitchen and threw back a couple of Tylenol, then decided to make eggs while I was up. Before I knew it I had a stack of pamphlets and maps spread over the kitchen table and was scribbling down notes on anything I might be asked in regards to our itinerary. Lillooet, Williams Lake, Barkerville, Quesnel . . . historical facts, modern facts . . . local populations, First Nation's culture, resources . . .

"Whoa," Cole said over my shoulder, munching on a burrito the size of a pencil case. "You got homework, kangaroo?"

"Call me that again and I'll deck you, moose." I checked the time. Nearly midnight already. "When did you get back?"

Cole shrugged. "No idea."

I packed my things away. "You'll have the place to yourself next week, by the way. I've got my first real tour."

"You're still paying rent though, right?"

"Yeah, don't worry." I sighed and stretched. "Good night."

"Night." He picked a bean out of his burrito and crushed it between his fingers. "Just so you know, Mexican food makes me crap like crazy, so—"

"*Good night*, Cole."

I locked my door behind me and returned to my bed. In Australia, I'd had a massive room with a balcony overlooking a canal. This place had a window you couldn't squeeze a cat through and an air conditioning unit that only expelled air stinking of fumes.

Positive vibes. Happy place.

So when I closed my eyes, my dreams were filled with heat and bushland and endless beaches, as far away from this dank little flat as it was possible to get.

Chapter Two

I SLEPT A GRAND TOTAL OF THREE HOURS THE DAY before the tour, mental checklists and doubts and stupid last-minute worries keeping me awake long after I'd gone to bed. My alarm woke me up at four a.m.

Urgh . . .

I threw a couple of frozen waffles in the toaster and selected some lively music on my iPod, trying and failing to garner a shred of energy. Then I got dressed in baggy jeans and an awful logoed T-shirt that was supposed to be gold but achieved something closer to mustard. I'd only been provided with one for the entire five-day trip, so unless there were laundry services in the sticks, it was only going to get worse from here.

Despite it being midsummer, it was still dark outside. A sliver of light was rising in the east, blocked for the most part by the mountains, but the streetlamps and traffic lights still glowed brightly. As with most cities, Vancouver did not respect the silence of nighttime. In fact, when I caught my bus, there were at least half a dozen others already sitting there.

The tour bus itself was leaving from a strip mall parking lot in one of the ugliest parts of the city, directly underneath a SkyTrain bridge and next to a business park that was big enough to be its own country. For people traveling here from elsewhere, it wasn't exactly a good first impression of British Columbia. The bus, at least, was nothing more or less than what I'd expected. A typical silver-gray coach sporting tinted windows and the garish logo of the tour company. The driver was already there, a portly middle-aged man with an olive complexion and sour expression.

"Crake?" he snapped, before I'd even crossed the parking lot. "You're late."

I glanced at my watch. "It's five-thirty on the dot."

"You were supposed to be here at five."

"Mr. Swierenga told me five-thirty. I have it written down"—I swung my rucksack off my shoulder and produced a slip of paper—"right here."

His eyes narrowed.

I extended a hand. "Lewis."

"Sergio. Sergio Macari." He didn't stop glowering at me. "You're young, aren't you?"

And you're old. Yet here we are. I shrugged. "Depends who you're comparing me to."

"Other guides." Sergio's lip curled. "This lot—the seniors—will grill you like a cheese sandwich about *everything*. I don't know what the boss was thinking, sending some Aussie kid who's looking for the 'Canadian experience' just as much as the clients are."

Taken aback, I stared at him for a moment. Then I gave him my politest, most innocent smile and said, "No, no, you're right. He really should've hired someone who knew that the exact population of Williams Lake last year was ten thousand, eight hundred and thirty-two, and Lillooet is precisely two hundred and fifty meters above sea level. He should've hired someone who knew that Billy Barker, who founded Barkerville, was born in 1819 in Fenland, UK, and unearthed around one thousand kilograms of gold in his lifetime, but still managed to die penniless. And that . . . "

It was immensely satisfying to see Sergio's cheeks turn red with embarrassment, and even more gratifying when, unable to think of anything sensible to say, he pivoted and stormed back to the bus. I hated how pompous I'd sounded, but still . . . sometimes, a point had to be proven.

The guests wouldn't begin to arrive for at least another hour and a half, so after stowing my bag in the luggage compartment, I went to take a look inside. The seats were blue velour, etched with those public-transit-esque squiggles meant to hide how filthy they actually were. Matching curtains hung from the windows, and an outdated television was perched near the front of the vehicle. Behind me there was a door leading to what I assumed was the toilet. It was pretty unremarkable, all told.

"They won't come for another hour, yet," Sergio told me, noticing I was hovering by the door with my clipboard at the ready. "They know we don't leave until nine o'clock."

"So why are we here so early?"

"Because rules are rules. This isn't supposed to be a vacation for us too, remember? The boss doesn't want us to forget that."

I waited anyway, determined to make the best first impression possible. The sun had been up for several hours before the first guest arrived, a nondescript septuagenarian couple who hadn't figured out how to print their proof of payment. Then, like they'd broken a dam, everyone else arrived in the space of fifteen minutes.

My first impression was that Swierenga had been right about demographics. The tourists were a swarm of white, gray, and thinning hair, almost all wearing sneakers and sensible overcoats and glasses with wire rims. They spoke loudly, as though Sergio and I were the ones that were hard of hearing, and either seemed to have far too much luggage or not enough. They appeared in a throng of disposable cameras, sandals and socks, ankle-length skirts, purple rinse, polo shirts tucked into belts, stooped postures, and shuffling gaits.

"And yes," Sergio said with cruel delight, "it's bad form if you don't memorize their names."

"That shouldn't be a problem," I lied.

"Good." He waved a clipboard in my face. "Considering this is your, ah, *probationary* tour, I wouldn't want to have to report anything negative back to the boss."

"He never said anything about a supervisor."

"You aren't supposed to know. I'm supposed to observe from the background, see how you act when you don't think anyone is watching, etcetera." Sergio leaned in close. He stank of relish and hair product.

"But I think it's better when you *do* know I'm watching."

Lovely.

I turned away to assist a particularly ancient lady with her suitcase.

I wasn't given much time to stew. At least half the group had forgotten or been unable to print their tickets, leading to more ID checks than an airport security barrier. There were several—well, more like a dozen—tourists with burning questions or concerns about everything from our itinerary, to toilet stops, to rabid wildlife, demanding my attention for massive chunks of time and refusing to let me go until I'd worded my answer exactly right. Some were polite about it; others treated me like a child. One man handed me a list of medical issues that was double-sided, and a trio of sisters managed to communicate that they spoke only very minimal English. They were mostly Canadians and Americans, with a few Brits, Japanese, French, and Kiwis. The youngest person I'd encountered was a sixty-five-year-old poet from Vancouver Island.

"Excuse me?" I was tapped on the shoulder. "It's half past eleven."

"There are still people arriving!" I exclaimed.

The lady thrust a watch at my face. "See?"

From the driver's seat, Sergio smirked at me.

Yeah, because only in this industry would the persistence of the guests be considered my fault.

The last couple hobbled up the stairs onto the bus, and I got Sergio to close the luggage compartment. Then, already feeling exhausted, I climbed on board, the doors closed, and we rolled out of the parking lot. The chattering stopped, and I was faced with a busload of eyes staring directly at me, waiting, judging, some kind, others narrowed, and some so mottled with age I couldn't tell the difference.

And that was when I saw her. One earbud in place and the other hanging loose like a necklace, long legs stretched over the empty seat next to her, and head resting against the window. Her hair had been dyed navy blue, scraped back into a ponytail, and she wore no makeup aside from a sweep of eyeliner. A girl about my age. Alone, on a bus full of seniors. How had I not seen her before? I must've checked her ticket. Had I really been so distracted?

She was avoiding looking at me. Nobody was giving her a second glance, like her being here wasn't anything out of the ordinary. If she'd been here with someone, it wouldn't have been. But there was something about the way she sat, staring out of the window with her jaw set like she was on the way to war, that made me intensely curious.

There was a cough, and I jolted back to reality. *Right.*

"Hello, everyone," I said, giving a wave. "I'm Lewis Crake, from Golden Tours, and I'll be your guide for the next five days." I spoke in an upbeat, jovial way, sticking to a script I'd rehearsed and maintaining a confidence that was trained rather than natural. "I'm from Port Augusta, Australia, which is about six hundred and fifty kilometers west of Sydney. Our driver, Sergio Macari, is originally from Florence, Italy. According to my list, we've got people from six different countries here today, which is awesome, although I'm sorry, I do only speak English." A couple of smiles widened. I continued, "Today we'll be driving from Vancouver to Lillooet, which will take around three and a half hours. It's probably the most scenic leg of the trip, as we'll be going along the world-famous Sea-to-Sky Highway and crossing almost all the way through the coastal mountain range. Um . . . yes, so feel free to ask questions, enjoy the views, and I'll touch base again as we reach different points in the trip."

A couple of wizened hands raised.

"Will we see bears?"

"Ah, maybe. Nothing is guaranteed."

"Apparently you *always* see bears," another tourist said, confidently.

"And deer."

"I didn't come all the way from Minnesota to see deer!"

"You *will* see a bear. They're almost tame nowadays."

I interjected then, pointing out that they most certainly weren't. The man glared at me, then rolled his eyes and began muttering to his wife, who appeared to be playing Candy Crush on her phone.

Eventually, as we shifted from the snail-paced crawl past identical bridges and buildings and into the mountains, everyone grew too distracted by the view and stopped asking questions. The muscles in my jaw aching from maintaining a smile, I took a seat right in the front row and exhaled. I considered going to sit next to the girl, but thought better of it.

It really was quite spectacular. On our left, there was the ocean, the same brilliant shade of blue as the summer sky, wrapping around the dozens of treed islands drifting in and out of a haze settled on the horizon. On our right, there was the mountain range itself, composed of lush cedar forests and sheer rock faces sliced by the highway.

This isn't supposed to be a vacation for us too, remember? The boss doesn't want us to forget that.

Part of my application profile had claimed I never

felt traffic sickness, so despite hating the sensation of reading in a moving vehicle, I took all my paperwork from my bag and thumbed through it. The hotel in Lillooet was confirmed, as was the local guide, and I'd compiled a list of restaurants to check out. The weather was looking good, traffic report was all clear, and I'd pretty much memorized the tourism leaflet for the region already . . .

I stopped flipping through when I came to the guest list. It had all the names, ages, addresses, phone numbers, contacts, and health and dietary concerns for everyone on the bus.

Wilson, Hera (F). Home address: North Vancouver (no street name provided). Phone number: not provided. No allergies, no medication, no dietary restrictions. Emergency contact: not provided. Amount paid in full, July 3. Age 17.

That was her, all right. Hera Wilson. It was typical of Swierenga—or, technically, Rachelle—to allow a client to register without filling out all the information as well as being underage. I knew that as a general rule, no one under eighteen was supposed to be on these trips without an accompanying adult. And, perhaps more interestingly, she'd only paid three days ago. Considering she lived in Vancouver, it looked like a very last-minute decision.

As discretely as possible, I turned to peer at her again. Both earbuds were in now, her eyes glued on the scenery. It was, without question, odd.

"What are you running away from?" Chrissy had asked me when I announced my plans to fly halfway across the world instead of attending university.

"Nothing," I'd said. "Stop reading into everything."

She'd raised an eyebrow, glaring. "Please. You don't just decide on a whim to do mad things like that."

Arguably, this trip wasn't "mad," but there was one glaring similarity: it wasn't the type of activity young people just woke up and decided to do. Not alone, anyway.

"Hello." A woman who could've easily been born in the 1800s tapped me on my shoulder from the row behind me. She was wearing an old-fashioned poodle skirt and war-era blouse, her white hair in curls so tight they pressed right into her skull—a real mismatch of decades.

I blinked, wracking my brain to try and recall her name.

"Jess Cartwright," she said, helpfully. "You may recognize me from James Bond. Have you ever heard of Washington? Not the capital, the state. That's where I'm from. Not Hollywood, but that doesn't mean I can't be famous. You look like you might be famous."

Her companion was a woman in her late sixties, dressed to blend in, and carried enough facial similarities that I took her to be Jess's daughter. She gave me an apologetic wince.

Smile function: on.

"Which film were you in?" I asked, putting away my papers.

"Are you deaf, boy?" She smirked at her daughter. "James Bond. I already told you."

And so went the next several hours.

Chapter Three

SWIERENGA NEEDN'T HAVE WORRIED THAT I'D END up on a holiday myself. The only thing that freed me from Jess's ridiculous nattering was pressure from other passengers to share my attention with the entire bus. I was asked questions about things so obscure even Google couldn't be of help, and I nearly lost my temper with a woman who was adamant we'd taken a slow route on purpose.

"I live right here! I'm a local!" she insisted. "Born and raised in the valley. And I'd bet, well, my *life*, that it would've been faster to head east first! This is ridiculous!"

I brought up MapQuest on my phone. "See, ma'am, there's a fifty-minute—"

She nearly hit the phone out of my hand. "I don't deal with any of that technology garbage. It's always wrong. I get terrible backaches if I sit down too long, you see, and I'm *not* happy to have a guide who clearly doesn't know basic things like which highways to take!"

Start walking the other way if you think it'd be faster then, you soggy old badger.

"Ma'am," I said, courteously, "going east would've meant driving straight through several cities in Greater Vancouver, as well as having to head too far in the wrong direction by account of the valley—"

"Which is where I live."

"—and I can absolutely, one hundred percent guarantee you, the northbound highway is far faster. And more scenic."

She snorted, rolling her eyes at me like I was a stupid child who still thought the world was flat. "You've probably never even come up here before, have you? You just tap away into your phone, shuffle your papers, and expect us to go along with it. Well, I tell you what—"

"A bear! A bear! A bear!"

Thank God.

I gave the woman, Grace Schatz, an apologetic smile that didn't reach my eyes and left to see what the fuss was about.

We were in the thick of the coastal mountain range by now, peaks—some of which were still capped in snow—looming up at all sides and making the bus feel like a toy. To our left there was a river, glacial green, crashing over rocks, fallen trees, and around the bases of mountains alongside the road. That was where several fingers were pointing as the shouts grew in excitement.

"A bear! Look, look, can't you see it?"

"No? Wait, yes, yes, I do!"

People were rising from their seats and fishing for cameras in a total and utter panic. I nodded for Sergio to stop. There were no other cars on this stretch of highway, at least. The woods here weren't ancient like the ones flanking the ocean; these were the logging forests. This, at least, made it easier to see through the minimal undergrowth and search for the bear.

I hesitated around the fringe of the group. Having lived in several cities throughout my life, I knew how to be aggressive when the crowds required it. However, the elbows-out rule seemed unethical when applied to a swarm of seniors.

"Can you see it?" A falsely blond head whipped around, and a liver-spotted hand adorned with layer upon layer of costume jewelry seized my own. "Right there, through the trees, a great big grizzly . . . "

"I can't see it."

"That's because you're blind, love."

"Get out of the way!"

"Take a picture! Quickly, take a picture!"

"I can't see it either!"

I shook free and stood on my toes, blocked by the gathered heads. By guy standards, I was relatively short, the polar opposite of all my six-foot-five friends who had noodles for arms and string for legs, and on this occasion, it didn't help.

"Is it a brown or black bear?" someone demanded.

"Black, the brown ones are at higher elevations," the know-it-all man, Doug Wimberley, replied.

"Aren't we at a high elevation?"

"Shush, you'll scare it away."

"I *still* can't see it."

Camera flashes were going off all over the place. I might have been leery about using force to get to the window, but the majority of the tourists were decidedly *not* so opposed. Several times I was prodded and shoved in the ribs, squashed in with the crowd like I was one of them.

"This is ridiculous," I muttered under my breath, ducking back out into the aisle. Then, louder, "Can everyone please try to spread out so that we all have a chance to look? Thank you."

Slowing down to their usual shuffling pace, they obeyed.

"Look!" Schatz shrieked at such a high octave I

wondered if there were cubs involved too. In my experience, nothing excited girls—therefore, possibly elderly ladies too—more than baby animals. "We can go outside!"

"Ah, no you can't," I contradicted, alarmed. "Not unless you want to be mauled or—"

"But look!"

This time, I was provided with a gap. Now, the majority weren't gawping at the elusive bear at all—they were pointing at Hera, who was standing by the side of the road all by herself.

"What?" I snapped my head around to glare at Sergio. "What were you thinking?"

He shrugged. "Sorry."

"Open the door again. And don't let anyone else out, all right?"

I ran outside, automatically inhaling a deep breath of the fresh air, a godsend after hours on the stale, perfumed bus. Then I strode over to Hera and tried to force all my earlier curiosities out of mind.

"You can't be out here," I said, cringing. I sounded

patronizing even to myself, using the same overly polite tone I'd used with Schatz. "It's dangerous."

Hera rolled her eyes. "I beg to differ."

Was this going to end up another case of as-a-local-I-know-more-than-you? Dangerous creatures were an area that she couldn't possibly fault me, as an Australian, for being ignorant of.

"Her—" I stopped myself. I addressed all the other guests as "ma'am" and "sir," not by their first names. But doing so felt far too awkward with someone my own age in comparison. *Too bad, sunshine.* "Miss Wilson, I must insist—"

To my increased surprise, she burst out laughing. "Ha, listen to you! What century are you from?" She grinned at me, then laughed again. "There is no bear, Lewis, don't you see? It's a *log.*"

I blinked.

"If we run," Hera whispered, leaning in close and resting a hand on my shoulder, "we may still be able to save ourselves."

I jerked away from her touch, back stiffening. "After all that, a log? They'll be disappointed."

She studied me. "Disappointed," she echoed.

I pretended to be interested in the log. It wasn't difficult to see how, at a distance, it could be mistaken for a bear; it was on the other side of the creek, obscured in shadow, and warped into an odd, animalistic shape. A banging on the windows behind us dragged me back into the moment.

"You really do need to go inside again," I sighed. "They'll never give it a rest otherwise."

Hera nodded. Her grin had faded away, now replaced with something almost like resignation. "Okay. Sorry. I just—"

"It's not your fault." I gritted my teeth and gestured for Sergio to open the doors again. "He should've known better than to let you out."

"No, it is my fault." Her eyes flickered to Sergio before resting back on me. "I asked."

"Well . . . just ask me in the future," I said. As an

afterthought, I added, “By the way, I was wondering about—”

But Hera had already returned to her seat, hidden behind a swarm of people still craning to see the elusive bear.

– – –

The realization that the bear was, in fact, a log brought a chorus of groans from the group. Many people insisted that they'd suspected it from the start, and the couple who spotted it in the first place shrank back to their seats, blushing. Hera didn't say anything, plugging her headphones in and frowning at the window.

It wasn't a complete disaster. We saw a herd of deer, several massive eagles, and a lone coyote slinking through the forest, enough to satisfy most of the tourists. We stopped for lunch in Squamish, a coastal town dominated by towering granite massifs, and progressed inland without having to stop again. Grace Schatz continued to throw stupid questions at me, Doug Wimberley continued to narrate with his "extensive" knowledge, and I continued to absorb myself in my papers. When I chanced another glance at Hera, I noticed she was no longer sitting alone; an octogenarian couple had joined her, speaking in thick French accents, and every now and then, they would all burst out laughing. I took it as a good thing.

As the scenery shifted yet again, I moved into the aisle and coughed for everyone's attention.

"We should be arriving in Lillooet in the next fifteen to twenty minutes," I said, met with a round of cheers. "When we arrive, don't worry about luggage. Sergio will take it to the hotel. Our local guide will meet us, we'll explore the town, then we'll check into the hotel, and you'll be free to have dinner or walk around as you choose. Questions?"

"Yeah." Doug stuck his pudgy hand in the air. "Why aren't you doing the touring? Isn't that what we paid you for?"

My smile thinned. "You pay me to arrange hotels, transport, attractions, and general logistics, *sir*. You'd be hard pressed to find anyone who is an expert in every destination."

He shrugged.

More questions followed, mostly about dinner, then I returned to my seat and the group broke into chatter. I searched for something else to do and, unable to find anything, copied Hera and turned to the window to take in the scenery for the first time. It was amazing, only four hours into the trip, how exhausted I felt already.

Chapter Four

LILLOOET APPEARED ALL OF A SUDDEN, ANNOUNCING itself with a sign and the slogan *BC's Little Nugget.* Here, the dense pine forests had thinned out, like somebody had shaved all the hills bare and trees were only just starting to regrow in a few places. We were bordering on a semi-arid region known as the Okanagan, Canada's very own desert, suggesting itself through foothills of sage, thistles, and rabbitbrush. It was like some odd crossbreed between the alpine north and the Californian desert, and the closest to home I'd probably ever get in British Columbia.

The main street—practically an alleyway by

Vancouver standards—was begging for tourists as much as their slogan. Most of the buildings were designed to recreate the wild-western style, with sweeping porches, wooden siding, and store names containing unoriginal cowboy puns; all were clinging desperately to an age that had passed long ago.

Everyone got off the bus, stretching and groaning like they'd been sitting down for days rather than a few hours. Our local connection, who I knew simply as "Lucy," was waiting for us with the same polite, almost-enthusiastic expression I myself used. She was in her late teens too, glossy black hair woven into a waist-length braid, and wore a black hoodie with the symbol of the St'át'imc First Nation.

"Are you a real Indian?" Jess Cartwright asked loudly. When her daughter begged her to shush, she cried, "What?"

"First Nations, Mom," her daughter hissed. "That's incredibly rude."

Lucy pretended not to have heard her, although I noticed her knuckles were white against her binder.

I couldn't imagine how it would feel to become an attraction in your own home.

Before I could apologize on Jess's behalf, Lucy introduced herself with remarkable vivacity and explained she was going to take us through Lillooet's Golden Mile of History, which, she insisted, was just as remarkable as it sounded. Then we were off, shuffling to the first attraction so slowly that Lucy ended up talking to herself before realizing and turning back around.

"This is Mile Zero," she repeated. "The Cariboo Gold Rush wagon road starts from here, running all the way to Barkerville. In fact, we used to be the largest town this side of the Rockies, but now . . . "

We stopped at a few historic houses that, in my opinion, more resembled the house of sticks from *The Three Little Pigs* than anything habitable. Some had been refinished, done out with white picket fences and 19th century settler furnishings, the timber beams still only questionably stable. The guests liked them, anyhow, fawning over how quaint everything was. The three sisters filled an entire roll of film with pictures.

"This is how I want my house," Grace Schatz told nobody in particular. "All cute and rustic like this. They don't let you build anything like this anymore. It's sad."

"Sans electricity, sans running water, sans climate control . . . " the French woman who Hera had been talking to earlier shrugged. "I myself am not so tempted."

Ambling down the road, we passed vintage saloons and modern fast-food chains, replica ox wagons and far too many trucks to count, and gift shops galore. Then a mining museum, a pile of rocks from the gold rush era, samples of gold nuggets, and a railway station.

"The Pacific Great Eastern Railway once operated out of here," Lucy said. "The acronym was PGE, which the locals used to joke stood for 'Past God's Endurance' because it went so far north."

"Or Prince George Eventually," Hera supplied,

citing another interior town. It was the first time she'd spoken all morning. "What? I read the pamphlet."

The last stop was a steel-and-wood suspension bridge, creatively dubbed Old Bridge. I wouldn't have trusted it to hold a feather, let alone carry a person over the rolling Fraser River below. Pictures were taken, then we were ushered back into town for a stint in a gift shop stuffed with local artwork, imitation jewelry, cases of smoked salmon, and maple-flavored candies.

"Overinflated prices for the gullible," I heard the French woman mutter to Hera. "They should be ashamed, taking advantage of old fools." Noticing something behind her, she sighed. "Like my husband."

He pretended not to hear and offered them both a piece of maple fudge from an embellished, gaudy tin screaming LILLOOET in gold lettering.

I considered buying Chrissy a dreamcatcher, then thought better of it. She had no time for trinkets. So instead, I found Lucy and thanked her.

"Ah, don't mention it. I've been doing this for like,

maybe two and a half years now? It's pretty robotic." She laughed. "The hardest part is remembering that everyone else is hearing it for the first time."

"Do you enjoy it?"

Lucy shrugged, fingers unravelling her braid. "Depends on how I'm feeling—and on *them*, of course. Oldies are kind of a blessing and a curse. Lots of questions, but at least they don't pretend to hate every second like the grade schoolers do." She shook her head and let her hair spill over her shoulders. "Your coworker isn't very . . . involved, hey? They didn't make her wear the ugly T-shirt too?"

It took me a minute to understand what she was talking about.

"Oh, Hera? She's a guest, not a guide." I frowned at my shirt and winced. "Is it really that ugly?"

Lucy giggled. "It clashes with your hair."

"Serves me right for being a redhead, I guess."

"No." She cocked her head and gave me a coy, sideways once-over. "More like sunset colors. Gold, copper, blond . . . "

A crash interrupted whatever my response might have been, and we both whirled around to see someone had overturned a stack of plastic shot glasses. Everyone glanced at each other, and no one volunteered to apologize.

"It's fine, it's fine," Lucy sighed. "Where the heck is Linda? This isn't even my shop."

I watched her stride into the employee-only area and returned to the dreamcatchers. A little triviality wouldn't hurt Chrissy, I decided, selecting the brightest one I could find.

- - -

Our hotel was situated right on the edge of town, providing an unobstructed view of the mountains. The managers confirmed all the rooms, clearly pleased with the boom in business, and after getting their room keys, the group dispersed to hunt for dinner. I was delayed trying to get in touch with tomorrow's contacts and left to wander about by myself. I didn't mind—if anything, I welcomed the solitude. However, I stumbled across the French couple on my way downtown and agreed to their offer to join them for dinner.

Robbie Deslumane was a bald, slightly stooped man of eighty-three. His skin was pale, crinkled, and translucent, stretched over networks of blue veins and the marks left by a permanent grin. His wife, Perle, wore a pink knitted sweater and a grumpy enough expression that it could've been his face turned upside down, her hair spiked like a pixie. Robbie was a cyclist, previously a national-level triathlete. Perle made the best fruitcake in France. Paris was, in their opinion, nothing more than another dirty city. Robbie liked hats, Perle liked cardigans. They'd lived in Paris, Orléans (the old one, not the new one), Algeria, Australia (nowhere near me, though), Ottawa, England, and a tiny town in Manitoba. Robbie once spent the night in jail for stealing apples in his youth. Perle may or may not have had a career in government intelligence.

All this I learned in the space of about five minutes while we waited for our steaks to arrive.

"And what about you?" Perle asked, kicking Robbie under the table when he made to tell yet another story. "We have been hogging the floor."

"Oh, I don't mind," I said honestly. "I haven't got anything interesting to say."

"That is what all the people who *are* interesting say." Robbie reached across the table for his third bread roll, only to be slapped on the wrist by his wife. He reached around, grabbed one with his other hand, and began buttering it. "I am always concerned when people are convinced I will find them fascinating. I rarely do."

"Really, I graduated last month, had no clue what to do, so I grabbed the first work visa offered to me and hopped on a plane."

"Nobody is that boring," Perle retorted.

"Your mother was," Robbie said, absently.

"I have a sister with a hundredth-percentile IQ,

and once I found a tarantula in my shoe." I laughed. "That's it, that's all."

"That will have to do, then."

Perle clicked her tongue. "Leave the boy alone, *mon Dieu*! He is in the spotlight for too long already, eh Lewis? And I do not think that is a natural place for him."

"I'm not shy or anything, I—"

"—just find other people are suffocating more often than not," Robbie finished for me, not leaving any room for correction. "Those past their sell-by date can be the worst. I should know." When I began to protest, he added, "True, seniors have their benefits. To beat them at anything, one has only to stay alive a little longer. That is how I always win at the Seniors' Games. I simply step over those having a stroke or heart attack and—"

"Robbie!" Perle kicked him again.

"What?" He shrugged and winked at me. "Everyone has their own finish line."

"And yours will be right now if you do not behave."

I watched them, amused. There was nothing doddering about them, nothing senile whatsoever, and no matter how much they nattered at one another, it was obvious two people had never loved each other more.

After knocking back three full courses, we all ambled back to the hotel in time to see the sun disappear behind the mountains.

"Well," I said, "thank you for your company. I hope you're enjoying your trip so far."

"Of course. And it really is our pleasure." Robbie rooted around in his pocket for his room key, adding, "We must be cooler than we thought, Perle, now making friends with both the teenagers!"

An odd expression flitted across Perle's face.

"I haven't really spoken with Hera," I said, hoping they'd perhaps managed to get her backstory.

"You should make more of an effort," Robbie suggested, tossing the key to Perle and straightening. "She is rather . . . taken with you, I believe."

"Who wouldn't be at her age?" Perle chortled. Then she fell serious again. "But . . . be careful."

"Why?"

Perle glanced around, smiling at a bellhop who passed by. When she turned to face me, the smile was gone. "Hera Wilson is not her real name."

It took me a minute to make sure I'd heard her right. "Not . . . but . . . are you sure?"

"No," Perle admitted, "but my job trained me to, ah, pick up on such things. For one thing, she only reacts to the name half the time. She forgets it is supposed to be hers. And she hasn't got a single piece of ID."

"That does not mean anything," Robbie scoffed. "My wife has not yet accepted the stifling normality of retirement."

I laughed uneasily. Perle retained her dead-serious scowl.

"Anyway, *bonne nuit,* Lewis. Good night."

"Good night."

The hotel room could only be described as generic.

A boxy TV from the early 2000s; a twin bed wrapped in plush, yellowing sheets; a window rimmed with dead flies and dust; a copy of some abstract piece of art that, to me, looked like someone had vomited color over a blank canvas.

Day One was successfully over. Tomorrow should be an easy drive, and the itinerary was one of the most relaxed.

Perhaps that was why as I lay awake in bed, for the first time in weeks, I found my mind hooked on something other than the tour.

Who uses a fake name to go on a road trip?

Chapter Five

Desolate didn't even begin to describe the next leg of our journey. The coastal mountain range vanished, replaced with the vast interior plateau region of the province. There wasn't much of *anything* out here. Mountains were practically hills compared to what we'd left behind. Towns were practically roadside service stops and nothing more. Trees were sparse. The world was fading away.

Passing time, however, was all too easy. The questions and competition for my attention didn't abate, but at least today, I was able to simply chat with a few of the more easygoing guests. There was William

Pritchard, the poet, whom I could only describe as quietly flamboyant. He wore layer upon layer of shabby, old-fashioned, and brightly colored clothing, like he'd been a circus ringmaster in his youth and never changed his outfit since.

"It's good for writing," he said, showing me a notebook stuffed with words. "Here's one about Lillooet."

After reading a number of his works (which were surprisingly good), I was dragged over to Jess and her daughter, Emily. Emily was a doctor, apparently, and Jess's only surviving child. She seemed relieved to simply have a normal conversation. Then, of course, I was called to the back of the bus by Robbie who had, to poke fun at Perle, begun trying to unscramble Hera's "alias."

"I don't know why my wife is not helping," he said with mock indignation. "She is the spy after all!"

"I am not a spy!" Perle hissed.

"Retired government clerk," Robbie corrected himself. "*Oui*. But if it is an alias, the name must be an anagram for something, yes? Like Lord Voldemort, or—"

"You read *Harry Potter*?" I laughed.

"Of course!" He looked affronted. "I am a well cultured man, Lewis, not a heathen."

When we arrived in Williams Lake, my first thought was that were it not for the gold rush, there was absolutely nothing to warrant a road-trip stop here. As with Lillooet, the main street was a parade of shops outfitted like a western movie set, littered with too many cowboy hats and rodeo references to count. I got the impression that unlike Lillooet, much of this wasn't done for our benefit.

Almost everything else passed exactly as the day before. Our guide was a pizza-faced guy about my age who made it very clear he was doing this job to pay for college, not because he actually gave a hoot about history. There was another PGE railway station to visit, so the same joke about what the letters stood for was given, another "historic" house from the mining days that would've been considered modern in Europe, and a more enthusiastically presented explanation of the town's proud rodeo culture. Half the time, questions were all answered by me rather than the local expert. And, of course, when the tour was done, we were let loose in another gift shop for what felt like hours.

For "free time," I decided to head down to the town's namesake lake with the majority of the tourists. It was exactly what you'd expect a Canadian lakeside beach to look like: clear, cold water; sand that was pretty much just mud; picnic tables galore; and a panoramic view of the wilderness beyond.

"Are you not coming swimming?" Robbie asked me.

"Blimey, no! The water's freezing!"

"It is the middle of July."

Realizing I'd spoken informally, I corrected myself with a distant grin. "I haven't got any swimming gear."

"He's mad," Perle agreed. "He acts like he's eight instead of eighty."

Robbie was the only one who did decide to swim, while everyone else sat down in either the sunshine or shade and chatted amongst themselves. Even Sergio decided to join in, parking the coach and opening a book without a hint of his "this-isn't-our-vacation" attitude.

Perle engrossed herself in crocheting, so with nothing else to do, I brought out my stack of pamphlets and thumbed through them with glassy eyes. I hadn't thought to bring anything for my own leisure.

A sharp poke in my side.

"You look bored out of your mind," Perle said, almost accusingly.

"No, I—"

She jabbed her needle in the direction of the lakeside. "So does that girl."

Hera had a book open in her lap, but she wasn't reading it. She was staring at the water with the same vacant expression I'd been directing at my papers, not even flinching when Grace Schatz started screaming about a snake.

"I'd better go and see if Mrs. Schatz . . . " I trailed off at Perle's glare, rising to my feet.

"You have been talking to everyone else all day. And trust me, nothing would make her happier, no matter how much she denies it."

"What happened to 'be careful'?" I asked, not sure how else to react.

Her lips twitched, almost forming a smile. "I am curious, Lewis. She won't tell *me* anything. Given your, ah, advantage, you may have more luck."

In all honesty, I was irritated at Perle and Robbie both for making what should've been a simple situation far more complicated. I didn't want to mess around with Hera's feelings, and I certainly didn't want to use them just to put Perle's suspicions to rest. But now, having even a normal conversation with her would feel like I was doing exactly that. Oh, and Sergio. Telling Swierenga I was being "unprofessional" with a client would no doubt be like Christmas to him, no matter how unfounded such an accusation was. But I couldn't just ignore Hera for the duration of the trip either.

And I was curious too.

Although she didn't turn to look at me, Hera's back straightened as I walked across the beach to sit beside her. She'd found a spot underneath a gnarled ponderosa pine, mottled sunlight creating a quilt of shade and light over the bed of fallen needles, near a particularly marshy part of the lakeside.

"Hey."

"Hello. Do you mind if I sit here?"

Her dark eyes flickered over me, then she gave a slight nod. "Sure. It's not as comfortable as a bench, though."

"All the benches are in the sun."

"Don't you Australians love the sun?"

"That doesn't make us immune to heatstroke." I winced. "I never expected it to be so warm so far north."

She closed her book, somewhat reluctantly, and leaned back into the tree trunk. "Welcome to the interior. My family has a cabin in the Okanagan, and in July and August, I swear it's hotter than Satan's armpit."

"Your family didn't come on this trip with you?" I asked, casual.

"No." That was it. That was all. A single word, carrying a hint of warning and a hint of pleading.

I tried another tactic. "What book are you reading?"

She glanced at the title page as though she'd forgotten already. "Some corny horror novella. It isn't very good. I'm more of a sci-fi person."

"Space opera?"

"Of course." Hera laughed, visibly relaxing. "What do you like?"

"I'm more of a true-to-life guy. Memoirs, biographies, journals, that sort of thing."

"How boring," she teased.

"Hey, I'm not judging *you*."

"Sure you are. Nicely, though, but still judging. You wouldn't be human otherwise."

"Deep."

"Thanks." Another laugh, light and genuine.

I cleared my throat, ever conscious of giving the

wrong impression. "So, um . . . how are you liking the trip so far? I know it's only been two days, but . . . "

"Loving it," she replied, with what I took to be sincerity. "The other guests are . . . well, aside from the bad apples, they're sweet. I didn't think I'd be so comfortable. I guess that deep down inside, I'm a grouchy old lady too. All I'd change would be having you do all the tours instead of the locals."

"The guy today was a bit wooden, but Lucy was all right, wasn't she?"

Hera's smile tightened. "Sure, I suppose." She twirled a navy strand of hair around her finger until the tip turned purple, and I wondered if she was one of those people who found silence awkward or one of those who reveled in it. She didn't say anything else, answering my question.

As the day progressed into evening, the light becoming golden and the dusky chill finally coaxing everyone out of the water, neither of us moved. A voice in the back of my head kept reminding me that I should try to speak to other guests too, but the more dominant part of me was too busy enjoying having a conversation with another teenager. Hera didn't ask personal questions or pry into my reasons for coming to Canada, and in return, I didn't dig further into her own backstory. It was all small talk, yet she had a way of making it feel like we were discussing the origins of the stars.

"Are we the last people left?" I glanced at my phone, surprised by how fast time had flown. "Last time I checked it was only four o'clock."

"Emily and Jess left about an hour ago," Hera said, yawning. "Urgh, sorry. I don't know why I'm so tired."

I stifled a yawn too, then laughed. "You're contagious. I suppose I better let you go and find dinner; I know *I'm* starving."

"Yeah."

Both of us stayed seated.

"You can always come out with me, if you want?" she asked, hesitantly. "I was thinking of just going to the local McDonald's or something, since I'm so freaking broke at the moment."

Yet you paid nearly a thousand dollars for this road trip . . . ?

"I've got to get back to the hotel and finalize things for tomorrow," I lied, without really knowing why. "Perhaps another time."

"Right, right." Hera stood up, shrugging on an olive-green fleece that was several sizes too big. She had her arms wrapped around her torso, eyes fixated on the reflection of the setting sun in the glassy surface of the lake. Then she pivoted back to me. "Look, Lewis, I want to apologize. I don't know what Perle and Robbie have been saying, or what kind of impression I gave yesterday, but I get that you have boundaries or whatever that you have to adhere to, and I don't want to get you in trouble and—"

"Slow down," I interrupted, startled. "You haven't done anything you need to apologize for." *Except maybe make this moment ten thousand percent more awkward.*

Her cheeks were tinged pink. "I just . . . shoot." She laughed nervously. "I'm sorry, I don't even know what I'm saying anymore."

"Maybe you're right. Maybe McDonald's is the answer."

"But you said . . . ?"

I shrugged. "I can make time."

"You're sure?"

"Mm." I stood up too, stretching out my arms and zipping up my jacket. "This nine p.m. bedtime routine is getting to be quite sad."

And so we traded the whispering ponderosas and lakeside sunset for the plastic red, gray, and yellow of the nearest fast food restaurant we could find, both ordered fish burgers, and slid into a booth by the window. The sticky remnants of spilled cola made the tabletop untouchable, so we ended up creating a makeshift tablecloth with our napkins.

"This is blasphemy," Hera mused. "Coming to Williams Lake to experience the old west and ending up *here*."

"Utter sacrilege," I agreed. "What's wrong with our generation?"

She grinned widely, showing a gap between her two front teeth. "Nothing."

Like at the lake, for a good while, we sat in silence. A radio, tinny and poor quality, blasted pop music several years out of date from speakers above our heads. Picking up the free Wi-Fi, my phone buzzed again and again in my pocket, but whenever I checked, it was nothing important.

"It was a social screwup, by the way," Hera blurted. "Why I came on this trip so last-minute. Stupid, really. My best friend thought I did something with her boyfriend, which was a complete lie, but she made a fuss about it and . . . well, why try to reconcile when you can create a year's worth of drama instead? So I signed up to get away from it all."

Huh. Perle would be disappointed. The more dramatic part of me was a bit disappointed too, if I was being honest.

"It's a shame this only buys you five days," I said,

unable to think of anything else. "But I'm sure it will blow over."

She gave a slight nod, unconvinced. The vacant look was back in her eyes.

It was dark when I returned to the hotel, but Hera elected to stay at the restaurant for a while longer. She didn't say why, and I didn't ask.

Getting ready for bed, I went through my messages with more focus. Oddly enough, there was a text from tech-phobic Chrissy:

There's a big storm heading your way. I hope you see snow. Be careful.

Chapter Six

According to the Weather Network on the hotel's TV, there was a storm cell moving inland from the Pacific that would hit the interior within the next few days. It was supposed to be heading south to the United States, but had switched paths at the last minute, promising torrential rain, gale-force winds, and widespread power blackouts. Or, at least, there was a sixty percent chance of that happening. There was still a strong possibility it would dissipate or change course again.

Today's journey was only an hour and a half, heading directly northward across the plateau to the town of Quesnel. Everybody had settled into the rhythm of things now, so luggage was packed quickly and we rolled out of Williams Lake exactly on schedule. Seizing my chance before the first round of questions were asked, I went to stand next to Sergio.

"Have you heard about this storm?"

"Of course I have." He wiped his mouth with the back of his hand, smearing peanut butter all over his wristwatch. "Why? Scared of a little rain, Crake?"

"We're heading farther and farther into nowhere," I pointed out. "Tomorrow we're abandoning the highway altogether when we go to Barkerville, and if we get stuck in the mountains, there isn't anyone out there to save us."

"You have no faith," Sergio scoffed. "I've been doing this for longer than you've been alive."

"If we need to stay in Quesnel a few extra days, I—"

"What did I tell you, kid? Stop being such a misery. You'll panic the guests." He glanced at Grace Schatz in his rearview mirror. "And *that* isn't the sort of storm I'll be able to help you with."

Resigned, I resumed the usual schedule. A happy, cheerful lowdown of what the day would look like, equally happy and cheerful replies to all questions, then a circulation of the coach. Another poem from William Pritchard. Another Bond reference from Jess and an apology from Emily. Nothing from Hera. Harassment from Doug that nearly caused me to lose my patience. A casual inquiry from Perle regarding my "talk" with Hera, and an onslaught of rather deep jokes from Robbie to make up for his wife's oddities.

Returning to my seat was like falling into bed after a tiring day. There wasn't much to look at—just the vast, steely skies and undulating hills. It was peaceful, though.

Well, except for the whine of sirens.

There shouldn't have been anything strange about that. However, when I did a quick survey, I noticed we were the only vehicle on this expanse of roadway. When I went to the back of the bus, I realized with alarm that no fewer than three police cars were trailing us with their lights flashing.

"What's going—" Grace began.

"Hang on," I said with a smile that came out more as a grimace. "It's probably just a misunderstanding."

I waited for Sergio to stop. He didn't. If anything, I felt we were picking up speed.

"Mr. Macari?" I probed, holding up a hand to silence another outburst from Grace. When he didn't respond, I stepped closer and hissed, "Sergio! What are you playing at?"

He wiped his mouth again and ignored me. The speedometer rose. We hadn't been speeding before, but now we certainly were.

The sirens kept wailing. The police kept on our tail, one of them gesturing in a universal movement for "pull over."

"Sergio, listen to them!" I snapped, tempted to reach out and grab the wheel myself. "If you're trying to get me into trouble, this is a really screwed up way of doing it. Pull over!"

He tapped the wheel with his thumb, whistling along to an imaginary song.

"*Sergio!*"

His eyes flicked to the rearview mirror again. Then, finally, he looked at me.

"What? Oh, sorry. Right. Pulling over."

I stared at him in disbelief. Shaking my head, I turned to the guests.

"Sorry about that, everyone. I won't be two minutes. Like I said, there must be a mistake or mix-up."

"I thought I hid the body better," Robbie said, quite loudly, to Perle. "Usually it takes them weeks to find it."

She didn't look amused.

A policeman had already gotten out of a cruiser, a severe man with bleached-blond hair and a moustache that resembled the bristles of an overused toothbrush. His partner remained behind, talking into an intercom, and one of the other cruisers circled around to park in front of our bus, completely cutting us off. I reached for my practiced collectedness.

"What seems to be—?"

"Officer Price," he interrupted, cold and sharp as a razor. "Are you in charge of this tour?"

"Yes. I mean, I'm their guide."

His partner strode up beside him. This man was bigger, bulkier, and bald. He didn't introduce himself, instead glaring straight past me at the parked bus.

"We're going to need to see some identification, sir."

With a stab of fear I wondered where I'd left my work visa and my passport. Aside from my Golden Tours badge, what other formal ID did I have?

"I'll have to—"

Officer Price ignored me again, walking around to the tail of the coach. "Your driver took a while to stop for us, sir. Any reason why?"

My smile grew strained. "I believe he was waiting for a safe space to pull over."

Price frowned at the deserted expanse of highway behind us, the lines of his brow deepening. "Right. I'm going to need to check the inside of your vehicle."

What was this, some kind of randomized drug bust? *Sorry, officer, the blazing hippie bus is already in Quesnel. We're the sweet little grannies and granddads.*

There was no room in his tone for negotiation or refusal. So, swallowing, I nodded.

An audible gasp rippled through the bus when the officers—armed, to make things worse—climbed on board with me at their heels. With some satisfaction, I noted the surprise on both of their faces when they took in the demographics of the tourists.

Price bent to speak to Sergio. I may have been imagining it, but I could've sworn he faked a thick Italian accent when replying. Price gave up and turned to me again.

"Were these people with you the entire time? Nobody joined late?"

"No."

"Is everyone accounted for?"

"Of course." Automatically, I scanned the seats anyway. Then I did a double take.

Hera was gone.

Price paced up and down the aisle, ignoring the gaping of the guests. He didn't seem satisfied. Passing by his partner, I heard him mutter, "It's a dud, Jonesy. I told them it was a stretch."

The other officer scowled at me until I broke eye contact. Then he nodded. "We're wasting our time."

Perturbed, I followed them outside again. Price scribbled in a notebook, then mumbled a quick succession of orders into his intercom. The two backup cruisers started up and drove off again.

"My apologies, sir. We had intel that a person of interest was on your coach, but . . . " He snapped his notebook shut. "She is considerably younger than most of your guests. We would have known her if we'd seen her. Good day."

"Wait," I said before I could stop myself. "What's her name? What has she done?"

Price's jaw twitched. "Do you have any possible information?"

I hesitated, then shook my head.

"In which case, with all due respect, it is none of your business, *sir.*"

I watched them speed away with a strange feeling twisting in the pit of my stomach. Exhaling through my teeth, I returned to the bus.

– – –

Hera was in her seat again. Both earbuds were in, and she was examining a broken nail with far too much intensity than was natural.

"'Social screwup,'" I quoted, seething. "Call me stupid, but I'm pretty sure 'social screwups' usually don't end with three police cruisers tracking you down hundreds of kilometers from home."

She pulled out the earbuds, blinking innocently. "Sorry, what was that?"

"You heard me. That was a lie last night, wasn't it?" I noticed most of the bus gawping at me. "Sergio, get us out of here. Now, please."

Taking the cue, he started up the engine and everyone pretended to resume their own conversations.

"You're overreacting." She rolled her eyes. "They never said they were here for me."

"You hid from them," I countered.

"No. I needed to go to the bathroom."

"How convenient."

She glared at me. I glared back.

"You have no evidence suggesting they were after me," she snapped, darkening. "Are you going to start unravelling my alias too, Lewis? Report everything you find out back to Perle Deslumane so she can analyze it? Do a background check?"

"I'm on *probation*. If this tour turns into a disaster, then I'm the one who gets axed for it. If there's anything illegal involved, then I could get kicked back to Australia." I took a deep, steadying breath. "I could've told them you were hiding. You owe me the truth, Hera."

Her hands were shaking. "I am telling the truth."

I leaned away from her, frustrated. I was dealing

with a different girl than yesterday, and weirdly enough, it was sending stabs of hurt through my gut. "I wish I could believe you."

"You can trust me."

I opened my mouth, but was cut off by a strange static sound emanating from her phone. Almost like . . .

"Hey!" she yelped, trying to snatch it back from me.

I bit back a curse. "You're tuned into the police radio frequency? Seriously?"

"It's . . . interesting," she said lamely.

"Whatever you've done, just . . . " I pinched the bridge of my nose. "Please, just don't let it interfere with the tour."

I tossed the phone at her and left to sit beside someone, anyone else.

– – –

It was during a stop at roadside services that I decided

to confront Sergio. Everyone else was either waiting on the coach or browsing the gas station convenience store, and he was standing by himself filling up at the pump. We were in the epitome of the middle of nowhere, surrounded by dark logging forests that sprawled for kilometers in all directions.

"What's going on?" I asked bluntly.

"I'm getting gas so we don't break down."

"I'm not an idiot," I said, stung by his sarcasm. "You deliberately didn't stop for the cops. Were you giving Hera time to hide? Is that it?"

"The girl? I've never even spoken to her before. The altitude must be getting to your head." He replaced the pump and faced me, black hair greasier than usual. "Now, I spoke to a colleague about that storm you brought up, and you may actually have a point. Things could get rough. My proposition is that we switch the Quesnel and Barkerville days, so we won't be quite so isolated if and when it hits."

I was so caught up in the recent police incident that

it took my brain a minute to change tracks. "Go to Barkerville today? But all the plans . . . "

Sergio waved his hand. "Forget the plans. You know your stuff, Crake, you don't need another guide. Anyway, it's that or risk getting cut off altogether."

It was the compliment that made me truly suspicious. "The hotels will need to be phoned. And Swierenga—is he all right with us switching the itinerary?"

"Sure, sure. So long as we bring everyone back happy, he won't care what we do." Sergio thumped my back and moved to the coach doors. "It's only another hour's drive."

The air was hot and muggy, and in the west, a patch of cloud was darkening the otherwise clear sky. It wasn't yet threatening enough to be of real worry . . . so why Sergio's change in tune?

Chapter Seven

NOBODY OBJECTED TO THE CHANGE IN PLANS, except for the usual complainers. I expected the bed–and–breakfast bookings to be more of a challenge, considering we took up almost all available beds the town had to offer, but to my surprise, a slew of last-minute cancellations worked in our favor. In fact, on any other day, I'd have found much to enjoy about the town. It was maintained entirely for tourists, with nothing modern about it whatsoever. Entry was ticketed, cars were kept outside town boundaries, the roads were nothing more than compacted dirt, and all the "locals" were outfitted in costumes dragged straight out of the 1860s. More than Lillooet or Williams Lake, Barkerville really gave the impression of entering another time, to the extent that I felt like a time traveler when handling my phone.

No, it would've been great fun, had the earlier incident not given me a very, very bad feeling.

I considered trying to contact Swierenga. The thing was, I didn't *want* to rat out Hera. But this was the test period of my job, and I understood how quickly things could go south if I lied to the police again. If I got my visa revoked . . . well, paying for the flight home would be the least of my worries.

Really, though, how bad can it be? You're overacting. She probably didn't pay a parking ticket, or shoplifted a pack of gum or something.

But Sergio was involved somehow; he had to be.

You've been spending too much time with the Deslumanes. This is real life, not some TV crime special.

Ignorance would have to be the key. If I didn't know anything, I couldn't be implicated. I couldn't spend time alone with Hera again; I couldn't keep searching for answers. Strangely enough, this only made me feel worse.

- - -

"This is amazing," Emily Cartwright told me. "I've never seen anything like it."

"It's reminds me of a movie set," Jess agreed. "Did I ever tell you, young man, that I . . . "

Zoning out and maintaining a smile, I let my attention wander. The streets stank of manure and woodchips, and were absolutely baking in the direct sunlight. We were shown saloons and watchmakers, general stores and jailhouses, post offices and museums, all constructed out of wood, all either original or built to mimic originals down to the last crude detail. Women in sweeping dresses and men in wide-brimmed hats grinned down at us from porches, so natural I wondered if they ever broke character.

"I love their clothes," someone said. "Reminds me of my childhood!"

This was met with a few chortles, until the local guide, a red-faced woman built like an ox, offered to take us to an outfitters that would provide us with our own pioneer garbs.

"Excuse me," Doug objected, "I came here for the *history*, not to play dress-up."

The guide looked at me. "Well, we're nearing the end of our tour anyway. I can take a group to the theater for a quick presentation, and you can take another group to the outfitters."

They mumbled amongst each other, deciding, then split into two relatively even sides. My smile thinned when I saw Hera join my group.

The clothes shop was like a little girl's closet, with racks upon racks overflowing with gowns, skirts, scarfs, hats, slacks, shirts, jackets, and any other type of historical clothing imaginable. Silk and linen and leather and flannel and feathers, black and pink and red and cream, sizes for children and sizes that could've served as tents.

"Perle would hate this," Robbie exclaimed, doffing

a ridiculous hat and wrapping a boa around his neck. "I should get my picture taken and give it to her for Christmas."

He shuffled off to do exactly that. To occupy myself, I helped the staff find outfits for everyone, or anything else that kept me away from Hera.

"Is that dress for you, Lewis?" Emily teased, nodding at a dress I'd been holding on to for Hanako, one of the Japanese sisters. "I think it'd suit you."

"I don't doubt it."

"You're not dressing up?"

"Ah, no. If I take this T-shirt off, I lose all my special status."

"You should." Another guest joined in, now. "Change, I mean, not . . . the yellow and your hair don't play well together, see."

I thought back to Lucy and sighed, "You're not the first to say so. However, nothing really does."

"Black would," one of the staff members piped up. "Sorry, I wasn't eavesdropping, I just happened . . . anyway, black would work on you. Would you like me to find you something?"

"I don't want—"

"Oh, go on, Lewis!" Emily's friend crowed. "You're the guide, of course you have to dress up too!"

"She's right," Robbie nodded wisely. "You really do."

Smile. You're enjoying yourself. This is all good fun.

So I conceded and found myself forced into a shirt with billowing sleeves, a black waistcoat, and tatty pants that were several sizes too big. Robbie found me an overcoat to cover up the ridiculous sleeves and a pair of boots to hide the flare of the pants, but I still felt like a walking pantomime.

"See, now you fit in!" Robbie exclaimed

"Finally." I sighed, that familiar exhaustion returning with a vengeance.

Robbie's expression grew serious. "Apologies, Lewis. You are tired." Voice dropped low, he continued, "It is okay not to smile all the time, you understand?"

“You look like you are the one who came from the theater, not me!” Perle, arriving with the rest of the other group, interrupted whatever answer I’d been about to give. Her eyes flickered between me and her husband, then softened. “I think—”

“Mr. Crake?”

I bowed out to see what the Barkerville guide wanted, head ringing.

After photos were taken, a grizzled older man gave us a different kind of tour, delving into the darker side of the town’s history. Gambling, rivalry, theft, murder, and all manner of crime ran rampant, kept barely under control by a host of ruthless lawmakers, one of whom was notorious for his love of hangings. We saw a graveyard, evidence of such an underworld, and were told tales of lingering ghosts that had some tourists paling. Emphasized by a wind whipping up and black clouds beginning to pool over the mountains, most people seemed glad to be shepherded back to their respective hotels. I waited in the foyer of the more popular hotel, and after a good few minutes, was handed a massive stack of gold-digger clothing to be returned to the outfitters.

It was twilight by this time, the sky prematurely dark. No stars tonight. It was a shame; out here, hours from the nearest proper town, the lack of artificial light would've made for brilliant constellations.

Something small and hard came hurtling through the air and smacked into my shoulder blade. I pivoted to see Hera twirling a top hat on the handle of a walking stick. She was completely dressed up in a red velveteen ball gown, honey-colored shoulders exposed and the untied laces of a corset fluttering down her back.

"This would make a great Halloween costume, don't you think?" She gave half a smile. "Victorian brothel princess."

"Certainly."

I kept walking, ignoring the pocket watch she'd thrown. There was something in her tone that unnerved me, something bitter. It was like she couldn't make up her mind, whether to act like yesterday hadn't happened, apologize, or get angry at me for whatever I'd done wrong according to her. As though, just like me, she could feel whatever façade she'd built start to crumble, brick by brick.

Well, not my problem. I wasn't hired to be a detective or a therapist.

There was a crunching of gravel, indicating Hera had decided to follow me. I ground my teeth and willed myself not to turn around.

"I doubt we're going to beat this storm, hey? It's a shame." She was being more conversational now, almost begging me to respond. "I wouldn't mind having to stay another night here, though. It's so nice."

I kept walking. The shop was coming into view now, white siding gone yellow and a sign at the door reading *CLOSED*.

"Lewis, c'mon."

Was two meters a reasonable distance to pretend to be unable to hear someone?

"What would Chrissy think about such manners?" she sighed.

I froze. I must've misheard her; I'd never mentioned Chrissy's name to anyone on the trip so far, of that I was certain.

Hera laughed without humor. "Gotcha."

"How did . . . ?"

She raised her palms in mock surrender, but her face was perfectly solemn. "There's nothing wrong with writing letters. I've always wanted a pen pal."

"How do you know about Chrissy?" I demanded. "And *how* do you know she writes me letters?"

Hera gave the ghost of a smile, just standing there in the middle of the dusty road with her too-big ball gown and blue hair falling out of its ponytail.

Arms burning from the pile of clothes, I set them down on a nearby porch. It was starting to rain, big fat drops smacking into puddles, and even the locals were inside. "What do you want?"

Silence, the wind, the rain.

Very slowly, Hera shook her head. "I used to be able to answer that question."

It all happened in the space of an instant. Two steps. A sharp intake of breath. Then Hera was kissing me, and the sky broke open.

Chapter Eight

IDIOT. IDIOT. IDIOT. I GLARED AT MY REFLECTION IN the hotel mirror, which was shaking from the force of the storm pounding the wooden walls. Or maybe I was the one who was shaking. *Idiot.*

Admittedly, it hadn't started out as my fault. I hadn't, ah, initiated anything, or given any signs that could've been interpreted as such. However, it had become my fault when I'd kissed Hera Wilson right back. Now, I couldn't even rationalize it. But in the moment . . .

I shook my head and went to close the window,

realizing my papers were starting to be blown around the room. It jammed halfway, so I left it.

So much for not getting involved, the logical part of me hissed. *Congratulations on successfully burning* that *bridge. Was it worth it? No.*

Yes.

"Crake? Crake, you in there?"

I jumped, crossing the room in two strides and throwing open the door. Sergio was standing there, his shirt semi-transparent from a combination of rain and food grease. He raised his eyebrows.

"Are you all right?"

"Yes," I snapped. I closed my eyes, took a deep breath, and said, calmer, "Yes. What's wrong?"

"What are the chances of staying here another day? The weather's only going to get worse, apparently."

"No! Of course we can't! You know we can't do that." I made to shut the door. "Nice try, though."

"I'm not messing with you, kid." A beefy hand slid out and blocked me from locking up.

"Scared of a little rain?" I said, mimicking his own words.

"Listen—"

"We can't change the plan any more than it's already been changed. Please, stop making this so bloody difficult."

The hand disappeared, and the lock clicked into place. After a few seconds, the telltale creak of floorboards announced he'd walked away.

Adults these days. I shuddered and resumed the pacing of my room.

Of all the possible hitches I'd prepared myself for, this was so completely unexpected I almost didn't know what to feel or do. Poor road conditions, nattering guests, medical emergencies, logistics fiascos . . . all things I'd made sure I was ready to handle. Falling for a girl who was a "person of interest" for some mysterious crime—oh, and who also happened to have psychic-like abilities regarding obscure personal details—was, without a doubt, the last thing that'd crossed my mind.

Admitting it to myself didn't make me feel any better. There were only three days left, barely a blink in the grand scheme of things. What was I expecting to happen when those days were up? What was I expecting to happen *during* that time?

Well, obviously you're incapable of just keeping your distance.

A headache beginning to pound the inside of my skull, I collapsed on my bed, wincing as the springs shrieked, and stared at the discoloration on the ceiling. The cracks formed something that resembled a massive spider or the skeleton of a snowflake. I tried to focus on them, but . . .

Stubbornly, my mind replayed the kiss again and again and again like some stupid scratched record. The relief behind Hera's burning eyes when I didn't push her away. My own surprise, replaced with something bright and *alive* that I'd never felt before. The awkward bulkiness of her costume, the biting of the rain, then a flushed grin before she was gone again, heading to the hotel to get changed.

Now, I'd had girlfriends before. A date to middle school graduation that had lingered into high school, a best friend who had later evolved into something more. But those had been slow relationships, picking up traction after months of hesitation and uncertainty, fizzling out in the same steady decline. There had been time to think, to consider, to decide, to fall in and out of love in a regular fashion. This wasn't even like those moments of fleeting attraction between strangers, something inconsequential and insubstantial; this was real enough to have me truly scared. I think it'd always been there from day one—it had just needed one of us to drag it out into the open, kicking and screaming, to make me admit it.

But I had a road trip to run, with two dozen other people who weren't Hera Wilson on board. And that meant, as my dad would cheerily say, I had to stuff my crap in a sock and keep going as normal.

Wonderful.

– – –

I was awoken by the sound of distant thunder and my phone ringing. By the time I'd registered the latter, the line had already gone dead.

"I reckon you'll be all right," the bed-and-breakfast owner said, serving myself and eight other guests pancakes in the kitchen. She was still wearing her 1860s getup. "With the storm, I mean. The Weather Network said it shouldn't hit in full force until the afternoon."

"You have a TV in here?" I asked, amused.

She winked. "And five channels."

So I spread the word that we needed to hustle and leave Barkerville as early as possible, then returned to my room, collected my things, and went out to check the coach was being loaded. On the way over, my phone rang again.

"Hello?" I said, the caller ID registering the number as unknown.

"Where are you, Lewis?" The voice on the other line was quiet, unsteady. Almost angry. It took me a minute to place where I recognized it from.

"Mr. Swierenga." I set down my backpack and took a deep breath. "We're about to leave Barkerville, sir."

"That's not where you're supposed to be."

"Ah, no, sir. But I was advised by the driver that this would be a safer option, given the current weather conditions. He told me you wouldn't mind."

There was a pause, and for a moment, I thought I'd lost the connection.

"Drivers do not have the authority to alter set itineraries, Lewis. Neither do you, for that matter. Unreliability is not a reputation a tour company wants to have."

"I thought—"

"Now, I do trust your judgement, Lewis. Really I do. But the fact that I'm phoning you at all should disclose how out of control you've let this situation become."

I frowned. "Out of control? Everything is in hand, sir."

Swierenga gave a sardonic laugh. "Tell that to the RCMP."

My throat went dry. The Royal Canadian Mounted Police were Canada's famous Mounties, but aside from their iconic red-uniformed touristy personas, they were the active national police force of the country. Whatever they were involved in was bigger than some localized misdemeanor.

"I'm not following you."

"They were waiting for you in Quesnel." Swierenga sounded weary. "They're after one of our customers, apparently. Unfortunately, now we're the ones who look bad, since I told them you'd be in Quesnel today and you quite clearly weren't. It looks like you're avoiding them." Before I could protest, he went on, "I'm not saying that was your intention. At least, I hope to God it wasn't. Just make sure you get yourself to town today and do all the sucking up you have to do, all right? And for the love of Pete, don't improvise again. Severing contracts isn't pleasant for either of us."

"I understand."

I held my phone in a clenched fist long after

Swierenga hung up, heart hammering and emotion after emotion pulsing through my body. Irritation, fear, resignation, anger, and—more than ever—a burning curiosity. I had to tell her. I had to give her one last chance to explain herself.

The air was thick with humidity and the promise of rain, and running back to town was doubly as draining as it should've been. I avoided the tour group as much as possible, directing a few people to the coach and answering a few rushed questions, searching all the while for that distinctive blue ponytail. I found her with one of the town's employees, a man dressed as a stagecoach driver, stroking his horse and cooing to it softly.

"Hera?"

She glanced upward, her smile fading at my expression. "What's the matter?"

"I need to talk to you. Alone."

We slipped down an alleyway between the saloon and the old blacksmith's, avoiding the gigantic puddles that had materialized overnight. There was barely enough room to stand facing each other, my shoulders scraping the timber walls of both buildings.

"I had a call from my boss," I said, diving right into it. "The RCMP are waiting for us in Quesnel."

"Us?" She paled.

"Well, presumably just you. No names were mentioned, but taking a wild guess . . . " I trailed off, gaging her reaction.

"Oh," she whispered. "Shoot."

"Yeah."

Hera chewed on her lower lip, dark eyes glassed over. Wearing denim cutoffs and a simple white tank top, she seemed much . . . smaller, somehow, than she had yesterday in that oversized gown. "I was hoping we threw them off earlier."

"So you admit it *is* you they're after?"

She gave a tight bob of the head. "I think at this point, it'd be useless denying it."

"What did you do?"

"Ah." Hera finally met my gaze. "That, I'm afraid, is classified." Her lips twitched into a sideways grin.

"It's far too much fun keeping you on the hook. I have a feeling the only reason you're keeping me around is out of nosiness."

"This isn't funny!" I exclaimed, despite fighting back an exasperated grin of my own.

"No." The smile was gone again. "I don't suppose it is. Are you in much trouble?"

"I mean, they haven't revoked my visa yet."

She nodded for a second time. "Good. How long can you delay leaving without getting in hot water again?"

"Technically we don't have to be in Quesnel until two o'clock, but if we leave it much longer we'll be stuck in the storm. Why?"

"Well, first and foremost, I need to change your guest roster. If I'm on it when you arrive in Quesnel, then it's game over for both of us. Then I need to disappear."

Disappear. Out here, surrounded by nothing but mountains and dense wilderness, anyone could vanish in a matter of minutes. However, given that running into the woods was practically a death sentence, I imagined Hera had something far more intricate in mind.

"But how would you do either of those things?"

Too deep in thought to hear me, she began moving out of the alleyway toward the edge of the village, where the coach was parked. I followed, but right when I caught up with her again, she stopped so suddenly I nearly slammed right into her back.

"Jess?" we said in unison.

Jess Cartwright, hyper-visible in a yellow rain jacket, was staring at us through her glasses with an unnervingly sly expression. Emily was nowhere to be seen.

"You were eavesdropping," Hera accused.

Jess clicked her tongue. "I'm deaf as a . . . well, I'm deaf, my dear. I barely heard anything. Except that you need time to make a getaway, that is."

We exchanged a glance of alarm.

"Mrs. Cartwright—" I began.

She silenced me with a wave of her hand. "I'm

offended you didn't come to me in the first place. You know I was a Bond girl? I'm an expert in all these things."

"Right. Of course."

Ignoring our sarcasm, she continued, "How much time do you need?"

Hera shrugged. "Maybe three hours. But Jess—"

"One hour of us seniors being bothersome. Easy-peasy two hours after we get stuck when the storm hits. And voilà, your one-hour journey is quadrupled." Jess winked. "I bet you're wondering how I know all this! I used to be an actress in James Bond."

Hera turned to me, eyes gleaming. "Would that work?"

I thought about it. There was no way I'd be able to stall for three hours. However, if we ended up getting stuck in the mountains while the storm hit . . . Yet, doing so would be incredibly dangerous. It wasn't like the majority of the guests had cell phones, and if the road conditions deteriorated, the chances of an accident was exponentially multiplied.

"Lewis?" Concern crept into her tone.

"It would work," I said slowly, "but you have to tell me what's going on, Hera. I can't risk all this not knowing why."

She waited until Jess had sauntered away toward the bus, then said, desperate, "Look, you could already be charged with obstruction or accessory for helping me. At least this way, you can honestly claim you had no idea what I've done. You have to trust me when I say I've never done anything *bad.*"

"The RCMP might disagree with that."

"Do you trust me or not?"

That, of course, depended on whether I decided to listen to my head or my heart. I'd never been much good at the former.

I shook my head and gave a short, humorless laugh. "God help me, I think I do."

She visibly relaxed. "Can I borrow your phone?"

I handed it to her. What else could possibly go wrong, anyway?

I watched her dial a number, grit her teeth when

the line went straight to an answering machine. "You've got to be kidding me, that little—oh! Hey! Listen, it's . . . yeah, yeah. Shut up and let me speak. No, I . . . I need a favor. *Pronto.*"

Chapter Nine

JESS'S PLAN HAD PRETTY MUCH ENABLED ITSELF. People were enraptured with Barkerville and reluctant to return to reality, so by giving in to a few last-minute requests, I managed to delay our departure by a solid ninety minutes. It was the rain that ultimately dragged everybody out of the shops and museums and onto the bus, and even then, Sergio took his time maneuvering back toward the highway. Ruefully, I noted the sky overhead was now dark as night, the rain pounding the windshield with enough force that the glass could've shattered. The wipers were on full speed, but couldn't keep up with the extent of the downpour.

"This isn't what summer is supposed to be like," Doug groaned. "Just our luck, this is the week the sun decides to give up."

"It'll pass," I said.

"I can't see out of the windows," he retorted, as though the storm was my fault. "They're filthy."

The highway out of the eastern mountains into the interior was quite narrow, and as slow as Sergio was driving, there was no avoiding the lake-like puddles lurking along the fringes of the road. The roof of the coach was already covered with sap from being parked underneath a pine tree, and the needles and fragments of pinecones were sliding down the windows in viscous, sticky rivers.

"It isn't a long drive," I replied to Doug, knowing full well that in these conditions, an hour was a very optimistic estimate.

"And we've got each other for company," his wife

said, glued to her Blackberry. "The view isn't anything but hills and trees anyway."

"Is it?" William grunted from somewhere behind them. "We could be in the plains of Tibet for all I can tell."

For the most part, everyone was silent, voices short of a shout silenced by the drum of rain. A few people had pulled their curtains closed and were dozing, others immersed in books or newspaper crosswords. I tried phoning my contacts in Quesnel, but to no avail; there was zero cell service out here.

"Hey."

I rolled my eyes. "Tread a little quieter next time, why don't you? You nearly gave me a heart attack."

Hera rolled her eyes right back, sidling into the empty seat beside me. "At some point, Sergio's going to stop the bus to check the tire pressure or something, and I'm going to meet my friend. I don't know how to convince the seniors to pretend they never saw me, but . . . "

"If you're not on the guest list and obviously not

with us, there's no reason for the police to interrogate anyone."

"True." She cracked a smile. "Thank you, by the way. I'm sorry you had to deal with all this. I didn't expect them to look for me on an old person's road trip into the sticks."

I shrugged. "It's my first tour, it wasn't supposed to be easy."

She hesitated, then said, "And I'm sorry about—well, kissing you. It was unfair, considering."

"Come on, I'm already up to my head in trouble. What's a little more?"

"You know what I mean. I'm going to leave."

"So am I." I shifted in my seat so I was facing her. "At best, I'll only be in Canada until the end of the year. We both knew that."

A sunny smile spread across her face. "Worth it, though."

"Perle warned me about you," I laughed.

"I am *that* girl your mother warned you about." Hera kicked her legs up against the seat in front of her, body relaxing. She plugged in a single earbud and fiddled with something on her phone. "Here one day, gone the next, getting you to bend the law in the process."

I eyed the phone. "Police frequency again?"

"What, out here?" she snorted. "No, this is Beyoncé."

A few people shrieked as a drum of thunder rumbled through the rain, then again as Sergio swerved to avoid hitting a fallen branch. It was the middle of the day, yet even with headlights on, it was impossible to see much. I had to keep reminding myself to let out breaths I was holding, the guilt for dragging us into this still not subsided. RCMP or not, it would be a relief to arrive in Quesnel.

"We had the most fantastic storms back home," Hera said wistfully. "They'd go on and on for hours. The lightning was so constant my mom used to be able to get dozens of pictures of it striking."

"Oh? You didn't always live in Vancouver?" It was

the first time I'd heard Hera give what sounded like a true account of her personal life.

"I'm from the prairies originally. Saskatchewan. Everything was intense there. The winters were freezing, the skies were massive, the fields just went on forever and ever . . . " She laughed. "It was so boring, you wouldn't believe it."

"You prefer it here, then?"

"Usually. Although sometimes the mountains are a bit, I don't know, almost claustrophobic. I miss the open space."

"You'd like Australia," I said. "We've got plenty of that. And strange animals, and heat."

"Well, I've always wanted to hug a koala."

"Mr. Lewis?"

I twisted in my seat. A particularly frail lady (Estelle? Stella?) was hobbling toward me, clutching headrests in attempt to keep her balance. Her glasses made her eyes even wider than they already were, like something out of a comic book.

"We're being followed again," she said in a

whispery voice. "I thought you might want to know. It's hard to see through the rain."

Exchanging a glance with Hera, I went to see what the lady was on about. Hera followed, movements becoming more tense and less languid.

Through the window at the very back of the coach, through a veil of debris and rain, there was the hazy form of another car tailgating us. Although it was hard to see, it did look expensive; a sports car of some kind. Not the sort of thing you'd expect to be used on a road trip in these conditions in a place this remote.

"You've got to be kidding me," Hera said in disbelief. "A *Lotus*? How much more conspicuous can you get?"

"That's your getaway?"

Her jaw was clenched. "Looks like it. I suppose I should be glad he didn't arrive in a zeppelin." Then her face fell. "This is it, then."

Somewhat dazed, I nodded. "Yeah, I guess it is."

The lady tapped me on the shoulder, anxious. "Are we in trouble again?"

Hera answered before I could. "Don't worry. Not anymore."

Sergio, finally realizing he was being tailed, stepped on the brakes and sent everyone lurching. There was a screech of tires as the car swerved to avoid rear-ending us, obscured by a tirade of confused questions being asked at the same time. Sergio "accidentally" turned all the lights off and announced he needed to check that the blinkers were still working, in which time Hera had grabbed her backpack and slipped out into the storm. She didn't so much as glance at me on her way, which was for the best. It would have only made things tougher. Heartbeats later, I saw the Lotus speed off ahead of us, and Sergio emerged sopping wet and declared everything to be in proper working condition. The lights came back on, and I returned to my seat, feeling hollow.

– – –

"I just want to apologize again for the delay, guys," I

said, cheery tour guide persona turned all the way up. "We thought we'd be able to beat the rain, but nature obviously had other plans! Despite the—"

I was cut off by a static buzzing that had people clamping hands over their ears until it faded away. Apparently the severe conditions were messing with Sergio's radio, and ever since he'd shut the lights off, all the electronics were becoming more and more unruly.

"Wasn't the whole point of going to Barkerville early to escape this?" Doug snapped when it went quiet again. "Some planning."

"I cannot control the weather, Mr. Wimberley. It's just bad luck, plain and simple."

"If we hadn't dallied so long in the carpark . . . "

A woman screamed as a tree branch slammed into the windshield and a thin, spider-webbed crack twisted across the glass. Sergio swore in what sounded like Italian.

"I have high blood pressure," Grace moaned, head

in her hands. "I *knew* I should've upped my life insurance before coming on this trip, I *knew* it."

"Look on the bright side," Robbie said, "if the bus crashes and we all die, it will probably make the news. Much more exciting than dying at home of a silent heart attack, is it not?"

Perle, mortified, cuffed his ear. Grace turned and threw up in her handbag.

It was impossible to tell where we were, the clouds hanging so low that it was like driving through sea fog. The mountains had vanished, as had all the trees not lining the road, as though the rest of the world had simply been erased. There was just us, the storm, and nothing else.

I watched the dozens of faces, no one except perhaps Robbie appearing comfortable with the conditions. Several complexions were green, many eyes scrunched shut, and not a single smile was being attempted. My eyes hovered on Hera's empty seat, then, not knowing what else to do, I brought out the dreamcatcher I'd bought for Chrissy.

"Did anyone get anything cool?" I asked, remembering the vivacity I'd seen when they'd been shopping. Sure enough, there was a rustle as half the bus began rummaging through their handbags and purses for their purchases, then a murmur as they all began comparing. Fool's gold, snow globes, T-shirts, syrup . . .

Just when minds seemed to finally be preoccupied with something other than the storm, Sergio slammed the brakes so suddenly that I, standing in the aisle, nearly fell right over. Grace started crying, insisting she'd pulled a muscle in her neck.

"Why are we stopping?"

Sergio swore again, this time very much in English, and pulled on the parking brake. Not a good sign. "Look for yourselves."

Like with the bear, everyone got out of their seats and swarmed to the front of the bus. Unlike the bear, it was obvious straight away what he'd been looking at: there was a tree, so wide I wouldn't have been able to wrap my arms around it, fallen right across the road. There was no way around it. We were stuck.

"What are we going to do?"

"Is there another road we can take?"

"Great. Just great."

"What are we going to do?"

Sergio coughed, looking at me pointedly. "At least we were luckier than those speedsters."

I followed his gaze in alarm. Right beside us, on the wrong side of the road, was the unmistakable shape of the Lotus. It had rammed the tree head-on, the hood crumpled beyond repair and airbags puffing up the front seats. Two silhouettes were standing beside it, veiled by the rain. One appeared to be shouting at the other.

"I suppose," Sergio said when I remained silent, "we should let them on board. That car isn't going anywhere."

"Neither are we. But yes, you're right." Was it terrible that I felt relieved?

After ordering the seniors back to their seats, I had

Sergio open the doors. Grabbing an umbrella proffered by William, I went to see what had happened.

Hera was wearing a burnt-orange raincoat that reached her knees, water pooling in the hood and running down her face. She looked furious. The guy she was yelling at was about our age, no older than seventeen, and was leaning against the fallen tree as though he hadn't noticed the torrential downpour at all. He had longish black-brown hair plastered to his head by the rain, eyes that were so green he must've been wearing contacts, and clothes that, despite being sopping wet, were cutting-edge fashionable.

" . . . how else was I supposed to cover a nine-hour journey in a morning? If you're going to be picky, then next time you get your backside in a fix, either call someone else or give me a few days' notice. Sheesh," he sighed. "If I'm going to steal a car, I'm not hardly going to steal a minivan."

"Did you consider *not* stealing? You aren't exactly poor, Janus." Hera glowered at him, not spotting me.

"I can't believe you'd bring such a stupidly recognizable car anyway."

Janus shrugged, unconcerned. "It was black, wasn't it? You should thank me. I nearly went for a purple Lambo."

I cleared my throat. Both heads swiveled to glare at me.

"Long time no see," I said to Hera.

Was it just my imagination, or was she relieved too?

"Actually," Janus corrected, "it felt like hours. How slow were you lot driving?"

"Slow enough to miss hitting that log."

His lip curled, and he offered a gloved hand. "Janus Ward. You must be Hera's stooge."

"Lewis Crake," I replied. "I feel the same might be said for you."

"Touché." He turned to Hera, a single diamond earring glinting. "You're garnering quite the reputation, hey?"

"Whatever you were, you're fired," she snapped. Then to me, "I swear, he was doing nearly two hundred kilometers an hour. It's a wonder we weren't killed."

Janus threw his arms in the air in exasperation. "What did you want me to do? It isn't my fault you blew our cover! I was good enough to interrupt my daily schedule—"

"Of doing nothing."

"—to come to save you. It's rude to be picky about it."

"I didn't blow our cover," Hera hissed, wringing the rain from the tip of her ponytail. "There was already a tip-off before we left, I just didn't realize. And don't forget, you owe me big time."

Janus gave a short, bursting laugh. "You mean with that jet? Please, I could've wormed my way out no problem."

Hera's eyes narrowed. "I mean Montenegro, summer last year."

"Ah. I suppose I *do* owe you. I nearly forgot about that one."

I cleared my throat again. "Um, could we do this

another time, mates? We've got a busload of tourists watching. And, if I'm not wrong, an entire division of RCMP waiting for you in the next town."

In sync, Janus and Hera glanced between the coach, the fallen tree, and the wrecked Lotus.

"I feel like this is all I ever say to you," Hera said, "but I'm so sorry, Lewis. That didn't go at all how I'd planned."

Janus's piercing eyes were still fixated on the bus, calculating. "Does Lewis know anything important? Or any of them, for that matter?"

Hera shook her head. "The driver is a client, but I haven't said anything to anyone else."

Sergio?

Janus gave a satisfied nod. "Then there isn't anything to worry about. Nobody ever speaks to the drivers. I can still get you all out, guaranteed."

"He's a brat," Hera whispered, "but he's also really, really good at what he does. Aside from driving."

"Okay." I took a deep breath, dying to get out of the rain. "I suppose you both better come on board, then. I don't know how long it's going to take for this tree to be cleared."

"Not long," Janus said, already moving over to the doors. "I called the Forest Service, they're on their way."

"How? There's no service out here."

"Rule number one. No questions. Absolute trust only, understood?"

Before I could answer, the doors opened and he disappeared into the bus. Hera reached out and squeezed my hand.

"I'll stop you from killing him if you promise to stop me from doing the same, okay?"

"I'm not sure if I want to agree to that."

She eyed the Lotus. "True, why not add 'murder' to a list of growing crimes?"

Letting go of my hand, she followed him onto the bus, me bringing up the rear. Janus was already lounging in my seat, flipping through my paperwork with a smirk, and I was left facing the rows of perplexed seniors. I had no idea where to even start explaining. So I didn't say anything.

Chapter Ten

"YOU'RE BLEEDING," JANUS NOTED, NODDING AT Hera.

"What? Oh." She glanced at her fingers, where her nails had been bitten down beyond stubs.

"And Lou-Lou over here looks like he's about to vomit."

"Lewis."

"Inconsequential. Does anyone have gum? I want gum." Janus leaned his head into the aisle and yelled, "Oi, any of you lot have gum?"

"I have hard candy," Jess called back. "Lemon, caramel, or lobster flavor."

Janus raised a perfectly manicured eyebrow at us. "Lobster? This, I think, requires further inspection."

With that, he sauntered over to her row and left Hera and me stewing in our nerves. It had been over an hour since the Forest Service cleared the tree. We were mere minutes away from Quesnel, and as far as I knew, still had no plan whatsoever about what we were going to do when we arrived. The simplest thing would be for me to kick both Hera and Janus off the coach and feign innocence, but I couldn't bring myself to do it. Quesnel was the only town for kilometers, and if they were barred from entering, then they'd be trapped up here. Even in the heat of summer, the northern interior wasn't exactly a forgiving place.

"Are we nearly there, Lewis?" Doug called, impatient as ever. The storm had subsided to nothing more than an unseasonal downpour, and now the excitement of being in danger was over, people were starting to get antsy.

I checked my phone. "Eight minutes thereabouts."

Janus, who had slipped back into his seat, nearly

choked on his candy. He spat it into his glove. "Excuse me? Eight minutes?"

"Um, yes."

"Then what're you still doing here?" he exclaimed, none too quietly. "Do you *want* to be arrested?"

Hera glared. "So you do have a plan?"

Janus glared right back, then stood up and shouted, "Stop! I think we just hit a rabbit!" Sergio stopped, everyone ran to the rear window to have a look, and he continued, "Now, get out. Lay low for like, a couple of hours, and I'll come looking. Try not to get eaten by wolves or bears or whatever."

"You're not going with her?" I asked, incredulous.

"Nah, *mate,*" Janus mimicked my accent. "I have to make sure a certain someone doesn't end up where he doesn't belong. You, I mean. In jail. Since my attempt to be a knight in shining armor apparently wasn't satisfactory, I've been reassigned to civilian protection duty."

"You'll be okay?" I said to Hera, a twisted feeling in the pit of my stomach.

Before she had a chance to answer, people began complaining that there was no rabbit, and Janus had to forcibly throw her off the bus before anyone noticed. It was silly to think nobody had picked up on her disappearing and reappearing, but all we could do was hope they kept their mouths shut about it.

Quesnel greeted us with a sign shaped like a gold pan, looming out of an area so flat it could've been the prairies Hera had described. It was weird thinking that we were nearly six hundred meters above sea level.

Relief was palpable as we pulled into the hotel parking lot, nearly three hours behind schedule. That relief turned to apprehensive murmuring when everyone noticed the police cars parked outside.

"Again, I apologize for the delay, guys!" I said, forcing a beam. "Don't worry, our planned activities will still be taking place after you've had a chance to check into your rooms. Sergio will take care of baggage, so make sure to reconvene in the lobby at four o'clock."

"Why are there cops?"

I promised to find out for them. The second I

stepped off the bus, no fewer than five officers rushed over.

"Mr. Crake?"

"Yes?"

A woman, petite under her bulletproof vest, craned her neck to scan the ogling tourists behind me. "We're going to need to ask you and your customers some questions."

"I'm just the guide."

Officer Price, with his unmistakable blond moustache, scowled at me. "We're aware."

I tried a different tactic. "Look, we're all exhausted. I don't want their vacation ruined by . . . whatever's happening over here. Does this really have to involve them?"

Price's eyes narrowed and he muttered something to the woman. She gave a barely discernible nod and turned away to speak into her radio.

"All right. You may offload, but make sure no one leaves the city without checking in with us first, understood?"

Single file, the seniors shuffled off the bus with curious frowns aimed at the police. Janus didn't even try to sneak past, giving the officers a sweeping bow before being immediately taken aside and questioned. Sergio, on the other hand, began unloading bags without being given a second glance. Much to my alarm, Robbie and Perle were pulled over after Robbie jokingly asked if they were here to finally nab him for his past crimes.

"Let's get right to it," the woman, Officer Barnes, said. "Do any of you know who Hera Wilson is? The name is an alias—"

"Told you," Perle muttered.

"—but we know she has been using it for a while. Seventeen years old, distinctive blue hair, mixed Caucasian and South Asian descent, five-foot-five, roughly one hundred and thirty pounds. She was registered for your tour, I believe."

"I have the list," I said, calm as possible. "There's no one registered with that name. I'm sure I'd have known her if I'd seen her, as Officer Price pointed out yesterday."

"Golden Tours' secretary confirmed for us that a girl with that name did provide payment to the company."

"Rachelle? She still thinks the sun revolves around the Earth. You can check the system, ma'am. There never was a Hera Wilson registered."

"Had it been any other crime, Mr. Crake, I'd be more inclined to believe you." Barnes sighed. "Perhaps we'd be better off doing this somewhere more private. All of you, come with me."

– – –

The room was duller than I'd expected. A florescent light bulb made up for the lack of windows, and a portable fan whirred from one corner in a vain attempt to cool the place down. Aside from a single poster outlining rights to legal aid, a table, and six chairs (the cheap ones often found in school gyms and community centers), it was barren. Totally generic.

"I cannot believe this," Perle said for the umpteenth time. "We are supposed to be on holiday, but because you cannot keep your thoughts to yourself, we are *arrested.*"

"Detained," Janus corrected, yawning. "Relax, my dudes. The only person here they could actually lock up is me. And I'm not worried."

"It's a story to tell the grandchildren." Robbie reached for his wife's hand, but she batted him away with an expression like stone.

"What? That their grandpa is a—"

The door swung open. Price and Barnes entered, the former holding a steaming mug of coffee that made the entire room smell like a café.

"Mr. and Mrs. Deslumane, can you come with me?" Price asked. He sounded as tired as he looked.

They shuffled out one after the other, Perle still shooting daggers at Robbie, and Price shut the door again behind them. Barnes came to sit opposite Janus and me, an impressive stack of papers straining to fit onto her clipboard.

"I'm going to give you the benefit of the doubt, Mr. Crake," she said. Her voice sounded too husky for such a small person, and I wondered if perhaps she'd been a smoker. Nervous as I was, such details were much more apparent than usual. "We've done a background check, and we've decided it's highly unlikely you know quite what you've gotten yourself into. You, however," she glanced at Janus, "appear not to exist in our system. So for you, I'm going to assume the opposite."

Janus maintained a perfect poker face. "Why interview us together, then?"

"This is Quesnel." Barnes cracked an almost-smile. "We're not exactly spoiled for space. Also, I'm hoping you may be so kind as to correct me if I go wrong explaining our situation to Mr. Crake."

Janus mimed drawing a halo, checked his watch, and soured.

"Are you familiar with the term 'cybercrime'?"

Barnes asked me. When I nodded, she continued, "Most teenagers are. It's seen a substantial spike in the past few years. We were alerted to a suspected ring of cybercriminals based out of Vancouver a couple of years back, but unfortunately, they were very good at covering their footprints. No traces. No hints. Just coordinated cyberattacks and IDs that lead to dead ends."

It made sense. The mysterious clearing of the hotel bookings in Barkerville; how she'd known about Chrissy; how she'd been able to add and remove herself so easily to the tour registration . . .

"Hacking can be much more serious than leaving funny Facebook statuses on strangers' accounts," Barnes went on, as though I was twelve. "This particular ring is thought to be responsible for the disappearance of millions of dollars and the leaking of confidential corporate information. Hera Wilson is the first name we've ever managed to attain. She also completed one of the largest attacks yet, stealing more than ten million dollars as well as files not intended for the public eye. The VPD tracked her to her house, but lost her. Then she resurfaced in your tour company's database."

"How'd you get the name?" Janus asked, casually. If I wasn't mistaken, a flash of surprise had darted across his expression when she mentioned the stolen money.

Barnes ignored him, focusing on me. "You see, Mr. Crake, it is absolutely vital we recover both Wilson and the materials she stole. We need your cooperation."

"I already told you," I managed to say. "I don't know anything. The youngest person on my tour is sixty-five years old."

"And him?"

"He was stranded in the storm."

Barnes studied Janus, taking in the designer clothes, the diamonds, the lordly cockiness. The fact that the Forest Service were still puzzling over the wrecked Lotus probably wasn't helping his cause. "What's your *real* name?"

"Courtney Branham."

Barnes asked him to spell it, then rose to her feet. "I'm going to run your name through our system. Have a think, Mr. Crake, if perhaps you forgot anything. I wouldn't want to have to double check with your guests."

"Are we off-the-record?" Janus demanded. When she nodded, he relaxed and waved her away like she was a clingy servant.

"Courtney?" I said when the door clicked.

Janus chuckled. "Yeah. I forget what he churns up, but it usually keeps them busy for a bit. If they get my name, they get the code, and the ring will have my backside."

"Code?"

"Classical god for a first name, common W surname. Helps us recognize each other."

Divinity and mundanity rolled into one name. I'd never made the connection.

I twiddled my thumbs and listened to the fan, acutely aware of how stuffy the room was. I hadn't felt this brain-dead since taking my eleventh-grade calculus exam. Either I told them the truth and betrayed Hera, or I lied and risked deportation. I couldn't see an easy way out.

"Listen." Janus grabbed my upper arm. When I made eye contact, he was uncharacteristically serious. "We don't do this for fun, okay? We're not criminals, we're . . . what's the cool term for it . . . *hacktivists*. Some company was negotiating to remove the protective status off a chunk of the Great Bear Rainforest because it was directly in the way of their pipeline, so Hera was trying to bring it to public attention. People have the right to know about this stuff."

"Ten million dollars, though?"

For the first time, Janus faltered.

"I don't know," he admitted. "The guy we work for, Pater, is hugely strict about that sort of thing, and Hera never . . . " He sighed. "She must have had good reason."

But the law was the law. Details like these wouldn't matter when it came down to it.

Janus must've sensed my hesitation, leaning in closer and insisting, "Hera came from the gutter, Lou-Lou. Her parents were killed when she was a kid, and no one came forward to help her. We were all unwanted, one way or another. Kids who fell between the cracks, who could either disappear or make ourselves disappear so we could get on with our lives on our own terms. If the ring hadn't seen our talent and picked us up, we'd be nothing. Sure, we work for hire, but that's just so we can eat and sleep comfortably. We're veritable angels, trust me."

"You stole a sports car."

Janus chuckled again, darker this time. "I tend to take on more, well, let's just say 'gray area' commissions than the others. I can pay the guy back many, many times over. But it isn't me we're trying to save here."

"No." I let my head fall into my hands. "Thank goodness."

He pushed his chair back, turned the fan onto a higher setting, and sat cross-legged on top of the table while rolling his shirtsleeves up to his elbows. “So. I’d guess we have a few minutes still before Barnsey comes to tear me apart. Want to hear my plan?”

“Depends. Is it very good?”

Janus winked. “I said I had a plan. Let’s leave it at that.”

Chapter Eleven

Sandwiched between an industrial estate and a patch of newly replanted forest, I found the group clustered around a trough with tin trays clutched in their hands. The shadows were long this late in the evening, the sun still partially covered by the retreating storm clouds that hadn't been burned away by the heat. Even the local guide fell silent when I approached, pausing halfway through a gold-panning demonstration.

"Where were you?" Doug demanded.

"There was a bit of trouble with my computer," I said tiredly. "I'm sorry."

Perle and Robbie held my gaze for a moment longer than everyone else, their eyes dancing with questions, only looking away when I gave a tight shake of the head.

I sat back and watched as everyone swished their silt-filled pans in the trough, groaning in disappointment whenever they found nothing but rocks. Jess gave an excited shriek when she thought she'd come across a nugget, and didn't calm down even after it was pointed out to be just a shiny pebble. When they were engrossed enough to lose any interest in me, I slipped away to find Sergio. He sat on a bench eating a hot dog, greasy fingers sifting through a bucket of semi-precious stones he'd bought from the gift shop.

"Crake?" He did a double take. "You were gone hours. I thought they'd actually nabbed you for something."

"What did you hire her for?"

Sergio blinked, tongue running along his lower lip in search of stray mustard. "What?"

"Hera. She said you were a client."

"Ah. My license expired, and she fixed it for me. No charge. I was just supposed to help out whenever I could." He paused, confused. "Where's the other kid?"

"Janus?" I gave a hollow laugh. "Awaiting his trial date. He claimed he was the one responsible for pretty much everything."

"They believed that?"

I nodded, sitting down beside him on the bench. My head was still ringing, and I couldn't imagine facing the tourists with a cheery face tomorrow. Now that all my nerves had fizzled out, I just felt drained. Like I was back in the apartment with Cole again, and the world was dull and heartless and both too big and too small at the same time.

"You saw him," I sighed. "He could pass for a girl no problem. Claimed Hera was an alias of his, that he'd since dyed his hair, etcetera. Their description was only based on a tip-off, so . . . "

"They took it," Sergio finished for me. "Wow. That was selfless of him."

I bobbed my head, but didn't reply. Whatever sort

of debt he owed Hera, I'd still been surprised that someone as self-absorbed as Janus would sacrifice years of freedom on her behalf. Besides, Hera had claimed he'd been an excellent escape artist, and as far as I could see, turning himself in wasn't exactly a brilliant escape plan. Still, I was off scot-free, and I supposed that counted for something.

"What about the girl? She's stranded out of town, isn't she?"

Don't go back for Hera, okay? Stick to your itinerary, finish the trip as planned. Don't go back for her.

"As far as we're concerned," I said as coldly as possible, "Hera Wilson doesn't, and never did, exist."

– – –

Bright and early the next morning, the bus was once again loaded and prepped for our two-and-a-half hour journey southward to 100 Mile House. We were retracing our steps now, heading to towns we'd already driven through to see things far less exciting than what we'd already seen. Williams Lake became a blip in the scenery as we passed through it, and I was reminded of how things had changed since then. How odd to think it was only three days ago.

100 Mile House made every other town so far look like a bustling metropolis. There was an eerie silence when we unloaded at a ranch, with only the distant chirping of birds and gurgle of a creek for background noise.

"I mean, given the name, I never expected much else," Grace noted.

"It's quaint," William nodded.

"Yes. Very provincial."

"Gets me all nostalgic."

"So laid back."

"What do people *do* all day?" Robbie gestured to the empty plateau, incredulous. "I would go mad!"

"This is a ranch, not the town itself," I reminded them. "But I'm sure during the gold rush, it was booming."

Our rooms were in a log cabin perched between the

stark contrast of the dark, dense woodland and sweeping tawny meadows. The only other visible building was a stable, easily bigger than the cabin, surrounded by dozens of horses and a few creatures I took to be alpacas or llamas. The property owners were right out of a storybook, both wearing denim, plaid, and heavy leather boots. Our bags were taken and we were herded over to the paddock and sized up.

"Has anyone ridden before?"

A few people raised their hands.

"I was once a professional jockey," Robbie said. Perle didn't scoff at him, making me think he was actually being serious. "When I lived in England."

With the help of a few stablehands, each guest—with the exception of Jess and a few of the other less able-bodied seniors—was fitted with equipment and a horse. As the guide, it wasn't part of the deal for me to join in, so I just helped out wherever I could. However, when everyone headed out and the elder guests were taken by the woman who owned the ranch to see the alpacas being shorn, one of the stablehands tapped my shoulder.

"Do you want to ride?" she asked, shyly. Blond hair, freckles, maybe fourteen years old. The sort of awkward young teenager Chrissy should've been. "Mom won't mind. We haven't seen this much business in, like, ever. And if you keep coming back every other week, you'll be her favorite person."

"It's my boss you should be thanking, not me. But thank you, I'd love to."

"You're British?" The girl's cheeks reddened. "Wow."

Before I had a chance to correct her, she'd darted away to grab me a helmet, and, of course, a horse. Midnight black, several hands too big for me, with a gentle obedience about him that made me feel at total ease despite not having ridden since I was eight.

"There's hundreds of kilometers of trails out there, so don't get lost," the girl warned. "Quiver knows the drill."

Right away, it was apparent that Quiver did in

fact know exactly what he was doing. I barely had to touch the reins; he just plodded across the paddock and headed into the trails as he must've done thousands of times before. The other guests had taken a route farther into town to see some remnants of the gold rush, so heading into the woods meant there was nobody else around. It was quiet in a way I'd never really experienced before, enough so that the clopping of Quiver's hooves became almost deafening. Every snapping twig, every snort, every time a lingering raindrop fell onto my helmet . . .

Finish the trip as planned. Don't go back for her.

Planned. It was laughable. Just like the idea of pretending none of it had ever happened.

I sucked in a deep breath of air, fresh and damp after yesterday's storm, and focused on the horse. The far-off sound of an eagle screeching, the spiderwebs hanging between the trees, the weird creaking of the saddle as Quiver picked his way through the trail . . .

Then Quiver stopped. His ears perked up, swiveling. Muscles tensed.

I tapped his flanks with my heels. "There's nothing around, mate. Just . . . "

Maybe it was paranoia, but I felt a flush of apprehension too. The unmistakable sensation of being watched by something unfriendly. But when I glanced around, there was nothing but trees.

"Hello?"

Quiver snorted and tossed his head.

Unnerved, I twisted the reins so we were facing the other way. There were too many animals with too many teeth lurking in the area for me not to take intuition seriously.

Out of the corner of my eye, I saw a human-shaped silhouette dart through the trees. Then there was a sudden noise like a gunshot, Quiver reared up in surprise, and I was slammed into the ground.

"So graceful. Really, I'm impressed." The figure bent down over me, their face a hazy blur. "No, you don't know me, but I know you. Boy, do I ever know you."

– – –

Maybe I hit my head when I fell. When white stars stopped dancing through my vision, there wasn't one person anymore, but three. A girl of maybe nineteen or twenty with dark eyes and a face that was all sharp lines. Another girl, this one closer to fifteen or sixteen, with a frizzy mass of blond hair that seemed too much for her tiny body. The third was a guy of the same age, who'd spoken before. And everything, from the way they stood to how they were looking at me, screamed *hostile*.

"What the . . . ?" I gasped, climbing to my feet and dusting the pine needles from my bare arms. "Who the heck are you?"

"Now why," the guy drawled, "would we give you such leverage?"

"Because you knocked me off my horse, so I think the least you owe me is an introduction," I snapped, irritation overcoming my apprehension. They were just kids, after all. None of them posed much of a physical threat.

The older girl blinked at the venom in my tone, scowl shifting into a honeyed smile. She'd been holding Quiver by the reins and, relaxing her stance, began stroking the side of his head. "We didn't mean to startle you. Sorry. I'm Diana, this is Sol, and that's Ersa."

The guy—Sol—glowered at her like she'd just told me an embarrassing childhood story of his. The younger girl didn't react.

"Last names beginning with W, by chance?"

Something dark flitted behind Diana's gray eyes. She exchanged a glance with Sol. "Well, I suppose that saves us all some time. Hera always did respect every rule except for ours."

Okay, so they were members of Hera's ring. If Janus was to be trusted, then these were people working for a greater good, so nothing to worry about. Yet something didn't feel right. The disdain with which Diana said Hera's name wasn't what you'd expect from partners in crime—more like from an enemy.

"Can I have my horse back?" I asked, reaching for the reins.

Diana's honeyed smile returned and she passed them to Ersa. "Sure. In a minute."

"We just want to know where Hera is," Sol said. "That's it, that's all. You obviously were in contact."

"Why?" I asked, suspicion creeping in.

"None of your business."

"Neither are her whereabouts."

Sol ground his teeth. He was a typical teenage beanpole, easily over one hundred and eighty centimeters, with the muscle mass of a garden slug. He wore glasses and was desperately in need of a haircut, yet there was a hardness about him that made me believe he was never a target for bullies. A little pinch of mania, maybe, boiling just below the surface.

"We've been following you, *Lewis*," he said, spitting my name like a curse. "Until you flipped the schedule, anyway. We know Hera was with you. We also know she never came into Quesnel, and we want to know *why*."

"We're concerned," Diana added.

I considered trying to grab the reins away from Ersa, calculating whether I'd be able to mount the horse before they had time to react. The answer, unfortunately, was no.

"She's fine. Now, can I—"

"Why do you even care about covering for her?" Ersa snapped, causing Quiver to jump again. "What's she to you?"

"We saw you come out of a police station," said Diana, maintaining her sweetness.

"I have an obligation to the tour clients. I can't disclose any information," I said, speaking faster than my brain could work. "Sorry."

Diana brightened. "Oh, we can fix that. If Hera told you anything much, you know getting people out of tight spots is our specialty."

"I'll pass, cheers. My horse?"

Ersa took a step back, her knuckles white around the reins.

I didn't blow our cover! There was already a tip-off before we left.

How did *you get her name?*

"You backstabbed Hera, didn't you?" I said with sudden realization. "You stole the money and framed her. The police never managed to track you, and after all those years of being so careful, she wouldn't have messed up. Someone must have leaked information from the inside. But why?"

Diana stared at me, stunned. Her hand twitched toward an object obscured in the folds of her summer dress.

She had a weapon.

"Look, bud, I'll ask you one more time. You ditched Hera somewhere between Quesnel and Barkerville. Where?" Sol demanded, edging away from Diana as though he'd also seen her weapon and was afraid of it.

Guns weren't legal in Canada without a permit, yet I doubted licensing was much of an issue for the likes of them. If it was a knife, I had a better chance of being able to simply overpower them, but if it was a gun . . .

There was nothing else for it. Either way, I was screwed, so I might as well attempt a getaway. Crushing any inhibitions about being rough with a scrawny girl, I yanked the horse away from Ersa and began running with him, wishing I could swing onto his back like the rogue cowboys did in movies. Quiver dragged me along fast enough that I wondered if I'd actually managed to escape. Then a shot rang out, and the world spun.

Chapter Twelve

My sister would have a fit, what with me always telling her boys weren't worth the trouble, then risking my own neck for a girl I'd only known a few days. *How am I going to explain it to her? She won't believe me if I say I was nearly killed after my tour got wrapped up in an underground hacktivism ring.* Typical, really, that that was what worried me the most during the moment—how Chrissy would react if something terrible happened—rather than the gunshot itself. Minds were funny things under pressure.

"You little *brat*, Diana!"

For the second time, I hauled myself to my feet,

winded after crashing into a tree. The bullet had missed, but Quiver, again, had startled, and was now circling back around with the whites of his eyes flashing. I knotted my fingers in his mane and faced the ring again, wondering if I was hearing things.

It was Janus, his face flushed a furious red. He had Diana in a headlock, leveling the barrel of a small pistol at her temple. Green eyes locked onto mine.

"Sorry I was late, Lou-Lou. I had a bit of trouble with the ranchers. Apparently good karma isn't an acceptable form of payment round these parts." He winced as Diana tried elbowing him in the stomach. Something in the pistol clicked, and she froze again. "Luckily my dear friends here made it quite obvious where you all were. It's such a nice surprise."

I opened my mouth and shut it again, too many questions running around inside my head for them to be properly vocalized. How had Janus evaded prison? How had he known to come here? Where was his horse?

"Surprise indeed," Sol said coolly, not making any move to help Diana. "I wasn't expecting you, Janus."

"I try to remain unpredictable."

"You can let her go," Ersa said. She, unlike Sol, was clearly uncomfortable with the situation. "We were only trying to startle the horse again. We won't hurt anyone."

"Please. I'm part of the ring too—we never shoot to miss."

A twig snapped a few meters behind me, and I felt Quiver's muscles tense under my hands. Nobody else seemed to have heard, so as subtly as possible, I peered into the brush. I was already expecting what I saw.

Hera crouched behind a large fern with her finger over her lips.

Are you okay? she mouthed.

I nodded. *And you?*

Fine. Janus came back. I told him you'd be around here—the rancher pointed us in this direction.

Perhaps fifty meters away, a pair of dappled horses

were tied to a tree, too busy gorging on a pile of apples to worry about what was going on over here.

"We're sick and tired of it," Sol was shouting at Janus. "They're a bunch of Goody Two-shoes—you of all people should know how much better life is when you're not controlled by their stupid rules!"

"What I do on my own time has nothing to do with the ring or 'their' rules," Janus retorted. "And I hate to tell you this, but there really isn't an 'us' and 'them'. We're all stuck in this together, and you know it. We've got too much dirt on each other to start cutting throats."

Sol snorted. "If you and that tour guide hadn't made things so difficult, it wouldn't have gotten so messy."

"So what? You systematically get everyone with half a conscious arrested so you can prance around and embrace the flash life?" Janus scorned. "I hate to reduce myself to insults, but you're a moron, Sol. You all are."

"I thought you'd agree with us."

"Sorry to disappoint you, but no. I don't think I've ever disagreed with someone more."

Hera watched this with horror, the sense of betrayal evident. Her fists were clenched.

"Your plan has more holes than honeycomb." Janus made eye contact with me again, then deliberately glanced in the direction of the tethered horses and back again. "I think the worst part about all of this is that at one point, someone decided you were smart enough to join the ring. Probably Pater. Pater's also a moron."

"Pater's next," Sol said with a hint of pride. "It's all set up. He and Hera are the biggest sticklers for rules—"

"More like a code of conduct of basic human decency."

"—and with them gone, swaying the group will be tenfold easier. Think about it, Janus."

Hera gestured for me to follow her.

What about my horse? I mouthed with a nod at Quiver.

She paused. *Wait a second.*

Is Janus okay?

Please. It's the other three I'm worried about.

I watched her, head spinning. I couldn't see an easy way out in the long run; there was no way to put Sol, Diana, and Ersa away without implicating everyone else in the ring, Hera and Janus included. Theirs was a system built out of paper, and if any one of them turned on the others, the entire thing would come spiraling down. All it had taken was a single name to force Hera into hiding—if someone went to the police with solid evidence, it would be game over.

Except for me. Officially, I'd done nothing wrong. Nothing that could be proven, anyway.

Very carefully, I slipped my phone out of my shorts pocket. There was a network of cracks twisting across the screen from where I'd fallen on it, but it still worked. Making sure to focus properly, while they were arguing, I snapped a picture of Sol. Then Ersa. I hesitated with Diana, realizing there was no way of doing it without capturing Janus holding a pistol to her head.

"Hey!" Ersa cried.

Janus smirked and, with a flourish, released Diana from the headlock. She crumpled to the ground, gasping, and I took a final picture.

"Watch it," Janus warned, not lowering the pistol. "I'm not feeling the love tonight, and I'm not quite sure how this thing works. I'd hate for there to be an accident."

Sol glowered at me, keeping half an eye on Janus all the while. "We'll come for you, Lewis. You better not have those pictures when we do."

"He's not invisible like us," reminded Janus with a weary grimace. "Sorry. You can't touch him."

"But *you*, on the other hand—"

I climbed back onto Quiver, wrapping the reins around my palms, and edged him down the trail at a gallop. Hera was ready on her own horse. Janus, keeping the pistol aimed, walked as fast as he could to where we were waiting.

"Hera?" Diana exclaimed.

Hera responded with a rude gesture, and with a sharp command, the three of us were racing back to the ranch.

– – –

They chased us as best they could without horses, but by the time we reached the open fields, they were lost to the dust. By this time dusk had settled, the heat was fading and the stars were glowing brighter in a mauve sky. The woods behind us were black and silent. After handing the horses back to the stablehand, who cheerily asked if we enjoyed our ride, we rushed to the ranch's dining hall in search of the guests.

"I doubt I'll ever walk properly again," Janus panted, struggling to keep up. "That saddle . . . "

Hera shot him an amused look. "It's your own fault for wearing skinny jeans."

"Why, you're right. How dare I not dress properly?

I should have known a simple carpool request would nearly turn into a flipping shootout."

The property had been set up almost like a hotel, with the cluster of cabins surrounding a larger long-house-style building. Dinner was included in the stay here, and through a series of glowing windows, I saw the guests sitting around tables, digging into country-style dishes. Hopefully they hadn't thought my absence to be suspicious. We tried to blend in as much as possible, slipping through the entryway with polite nods aimed at the hosts, making beelines for the few empty chairs. I ended up squeezing between Perle and Hanako, with Hera opposite me and Janus at the other end of the table altogether. Only a few heads lifted before returning to their plates.

"So you are back on board again?" Perle asked Hera, wryly.

Hera gave a vague response and began heaping her plate with fried chicken. Her hands were trembling so violently that she could barely hold the tongs. When I went to pour myself a glass of water, I missed the cup entirely and realized I too was shaking.

"Anyone would think you were as old and broken as we are!" Perle watched us, incredulous. "Did you have a bad time with the horses?"

"Mm, something like that."

Perle kept frowning, clearly wanting to push further, but was distracted by something Robbie said from her left.

Aware that others were also giving me not-so-subtle sideways glances, I took a deep breath and tried to will my heart to stop hammering. Everything was fine. Exposure should be enough of a threat to keep the rogue ring members at bay, and presumably Janus had fixed the situation with the police, and so there was nothing else to worry about.

Yeah, right.

Hera kept tapping her foot against a table leg, shredding pieces of meat away from the bones without eating any of it. She looked like she was as desperate to talk to me as I was to talk to her. At least it was as comforting a place as any, humming with dozens of scattered conversations and the wafting of aromas that at any other time would've made me hungry on the spot. A chandelier made out of antlers cast a warm golden glow and turned the windows into mirrors as the sun set.

"Excuse me? Who are you?"

There was a clatter as somewhere nearby Janus dropped his knife and fork. It didn't take long to see why.

One of the property owners had risen to confront three figures silhouetted in the doorway. A tall, thin boy. A small girl with lots of hair. Another girl, lean and wiry.

Nobody moved. I saw Diana's eyes shift from Hera, to me, to Janus, and to the guests themselves. She had the expression of someone forced to watch their parents embarrass themselves.

"They're not part of the tour, eh?" the rancher asked me.

"Ah, no."

"They could do with some feeding up, though," Jess pointed out. "Especially the young man."

It was too perfect. I almost wanted to laugh in their faces. *Go on, then, act all tough with a group of sympathetic grandparents.*

Ersa cocked her head and whispered to Diana. In sync, both Diana and Sol gave tight shakes of the head.

"Sorry," Sol said. "Wrong place."

"How do you make that mistake?" Robbie laughed. "This is the only place around for hours!"

"Apologies. Come on, guys." Diana pivoted and melted into the twilight, with Ersa on her heels. Sol lingered a heartbeat longer, eyes shooting daggers at Hera and me, then followed.

Chapter Thirteen

"I CAN'T STAY LONG. MY LIFE AS A FUGITIVE AWAITS."

Janus didn't seem upset by this. In fact, he was almost excited. "This is for you, Lou-Lou, to go with those portraits you snapped, just in case. I doubt they'll cause any more trouble now their plan has imploded, but it's always better to be safe."

He pressed a slip of notepaper into my hand. Full names, birthdays, addresses. Still nothing concrete enough to do real damage, but they'd already proven what damage a simple description could do. If all their personal details were dragged into the open, they'd have to go even further into hiding. No more parading about or whispering to the police.

"You know you don't have to do this, right?" Hera said to Janus. "It was *them* who stole the money, we could try and . . . "

"Please, Wilson, we're screwed," he retorted brightly. "My conscience isn't exactly clean, so if any of us are going to run, it might as well be me. Just make sure you get in contact with everyone trustworthy in the ring and let them know what's going on. Then disappear."

"But you—"

"I'm looking forward to it. I've got enough money to purchase an island if need be, and I've always thought I'd make a rather dashing outlaw." Janus bared perfect white teeth in a grin, daring us to disagree. "You just gave me an excuse."

We were sitting on the porch of one of the cabins, watching the sun rise over the paddock and wooded hills beyond. None of us had been able to sleep. It turned out Janus had escaped the police station rather than actually clarifying anything, but he wasn't concerned about it. He wanted to run, and he would do so until the police either gave up or were overwhelmed with more pressing issues, which, he guessed, shouldn't take too long.

"Right." Janus stood up, pulling on his gloves and buttoning a dress coat. This early, the wind was biting. "This is goodbye, then."

He offered a hand, which I shook. "Is that the pistol?"

"You expect me to give it back?"

"Please don't kill anyone," Hera said, only half joking.

"I don't make promises." Janus winked and leaned in, giving her a kiss on the cheek. "Jealous, Lou-Lou?"

"Shut up!" Hera shoved him away, laughing.

"I'd say pistols at dawn, but only I have a pistol, so it wouldn't be very fair. Don't worry. I rarely go for girls, if you get my drift." He was being playful as usual, but this time, there was also a sadness behind the admission, and I was reminded of his words in the station. *We were all unwanted, one way or another.*

"Go on, get out of here," Hera said. "And—thank you."

"Yeah," I seconded. "Thank you."

He shrugged. "I like debts in my favor."

Then, with an overly dramatic pivot, he vanished into the darkness. We hadn't asked him where he planned to go or how he planned on getting there, but I supposed there was no need. If Janus needed help, he'd find a way of asking for it.

Hera and I sat on the step for a while longer, wrapped in fleeces, and watched the sun lazily ascend. Today, we'd leave 100 Mile House for Clinton, and by this evening, we'd return to the car lot in Vancouver. *Then what?* was the question. But we'd already discussed what to do about Diana and her crew, and I'd seen her already discuss with Janus what steps she should take next. There were no more secrets left to unearth.

In silence, she slipped her fingers through mine.

They were ice cold to the touch. I put my arm around her shoulders, and neither of us moved again until we heard the guests beginning to wake up.

– – –

"So, everyone, we made it!" A chorus of cheers resounded from the bus. "We did hit a few bumps, but all in all, I think it was a pretty successful maiden voyage."

"And nobody died!" Robbie exclaimed. "Given the odds, that is something!"

This, on the other hand, was met with a round of awkward coughs.

It was sundown, so the mountains encircling Vancouver were tinged a soft pink, and a light mist was beginning to rise from the ocean. Given that Clinton only possessed a quarter of the population of 100 Mile House—my high school had twice as many people—our stop there had only lasted about an hour. We'd visited a quaint red-bricked museum holding relics of the village's once-bustling past, although really, I understood that it had basically been a glorified pit stop for prospectors traveling between Lillooet and Barkerville. And then, with a sense of deflation, we sliced back through the coastal mountains, passing the ski resort at Whistler and granite massifs of Squamish to arrive where we'd started five days ago. We were a few hours early, but no one seemed pleased by this. Despite Sergio opening the doors, no one left their seats.

"I'm so jealous of you, Lewis," Grace Schatz sighed. "You get to do it all again."

"Well," I glanced at Sergio, "that depends on whether I passed or failed probation."

Sergio pulled something from between his teeth and popped it back into his mouth. "Nah, kid, you passed. Extenuating circumstances, eh?"

"There you go."

The idea wasn't as terrifying as it had been at the beginning. Sure, it was all going to feel on the boring side if next time the clientele really was just a busload of mild-mannered retirees, but at least the likes of the Deslumanes had proven even they had their unconventional sides too.

"Can I just hide in the toilet and come with you?" someone joked.

"It's not the best hiding place," Hera said under her breath. "It reeks."

With the air conditioning turned off, it was the heat that finally forced everyone to leave the coach. Luggage was unloaded, and customer satisfaction surveys were handed out along with a brochure of other Golden Tours road trips. Unable to stand the baking heat of the car lot, a good portion of people shuffled off to cars and taxis as soon as they'd collected their things, but just as many lagged behind.

"Thank you," said Doug, almost reluctantly. "It was . . . fun."

"Did you learn anything new?"

"Not really, but . . . " His face burned when he realized I'd been mocking him. "Well, maybe. A few things."

After exchanging a handshake, he and his wife—who was, as ever, on her Blackberry—hailed a taxi and disappeared. The Japanese sisters, after each saying their thanks, followed soon after.

"Hey, you." Hera had her backpack slung over one shoulder and a sideways, pensive smile. "I guess it's my turn to say goodbyes now."

I glanced around. Those who remained appeared to be preoccupied chatting to each other.

"Where will you go?" I asked. It was oddly difficult to speak.

"Nowhere far. I just have a few loose ends to tie up." The smile turned shyer. "I do have a plan, don't worry. Unless it's what you want, you haven't seen the last of me."

"No! I mean, of course, if I could see you again, that'd be—"

Then, as unexpectedly as before, my words were cut off by her lips pressing against mine. But this time, there was nothing rushed or impulsive about it. It just felt *right.*

"Finally!"

We jumped apart to see all of the remaining guests either staring at us or cheering.

"I told you!" Jess cried. "Didn't I tell you, Emily? I'm so glad. I hate unresolved endings."

To my increasing surprise, I saw several ten dollar notes shift pockets.

"What?" Robbie gave a laugh, counting out fifty dollars he'd been given from Perle. "We do not always have much to look forward to, Lewis. Betting put some excitement into ending the trip."

"You . . . ?" I shook my head and returned his laugh. "You all bet on whether or not I'd get together with Hera? Perle, you bet fifty bucks against it?"

"I thought Hera would not still be here by the end." She shrugged. "Sorry."

"Honestly, I'd probably have bet the same way." Hera winked at me. "I'm not sure what made me stay."

Robbie and Perle bid us both goodbye, nattering as they got into a taxi of their own. Hera hovered a minute longer, then with one last wave in my direction, pulled a baseball cap over her hair and began walking toward the SkyTrain terminal a few blocks away.

"Come on, Mom." Emily steered Jess toward a waiting car. "We've got to get home. Cheryl and Patrick are coming for dinner this weekend, and the house is going to be suffocating in dust."

"Before you go"—I caught Emily's shoulder—"was she ever actually in a Bond film?"

Emily nodded. "*Thunderball.* An extra. She doesn't lie, just exaggerates."

Chapter Fourteen

It was a weird sensation. Like waking up from a particularly vivid dream only to fall asleep again and return to dreaming about something quieter. Sergio, under the condition I'd keep my mouth shut about his expired license, fed Swierenga a glowing report about my performance. Combined with the overwhelmingly positive feedback from the guests, he'd decided I deserved to be slated for another tour right away.

"How d'you feel about doing the Cariboo trail again? There's another one leaving Monday. We have a few that focus more on the Klondike too, if

Barkerville wasn't northerly enough for you. D'you know anything about that, Crake?"

Throughout the rest of July and into August, I took another four groups into the interior. The main demographic never changed, although the third time, a few families were also present. I ended up seeing several bears, and over the course of a month, the weather never interfered with our plans again. The largest hiccup was a woman's tongue swelling into a balloon after eating an oyster, due to a seafood allergy. Police stations and cybercrime rings were worlds away.

I found with each trip, I relaxed a little bit more. I got to know the locals, and my massive stack of papers was no longer needed. Falling into routine put all my homesickness on a back burner.

It wasn't until the last weeks of August that Swierenga called me to his house again and informed me my routine was going to change. In my spare time, I'd completed coursework on the Klondike, and apparently, the scheduled guide had broken his ankle and couldn't complete the last tour.

"I know it's a bit last minute," Swierenga apologized. "And it comes with an extra few tasks too. But you're one of my best."

"What extra tasks?"

"Training." He raised his palms, as though I'd started shouting. "Now, it isn't as bad as it seems. It's come to my attention that maybe our guides should actually complete a tour before taking control of one, so all you'd have to do is show a newbie the ropes. She'd take notes, you'd just be your usual charming self. I understand you haven't gone to the Yukon yet either, but you seem to respond well to being thrown in the deep end."

"Sure. A challenge would be good."

Looking pleased, he reclined in his chair and called for Rachelle. "Have you finished with the paperwork? Yes? Can you bring the trainee in to meet Lewis?" Turning back to me, he whispered, "You'll like her. Very quiet, very sweet."

A few minutes later, the "trainee" followed Rachelle into the living room.

"This is Melanie Torres. She's seventeen, I believe, Vancouver native . . . "

Swierenga's words faded into background noise. Because even though the girl's name and general appearance were unfamiliar, for me, it wasn't difficult to see through all that. *Hera.*

Outwardly, the biggest change was her hair. No longer shocking blue, it had been returned to what I assumed was its natural black. It was shorter too, and feathery layers nearly obscured one eye. Her clothes were different, though I couldn't place how, and there was even something changed about her posture. Less languid, more . . . shy, almost. She'd truly transformed herself into someone else.

Swierenga frowned. "Do you already know each other?"

"Ah, no. No." I regained my composure. "She just reminds me of someone I used to know."

"I have one of those faces," Hera shrugged. Her eyes were bright and her lips kept twitching into a smile. "It's great to meet you, Lewis."

Chapter Fifteen

Dear Lou-Lou & Wilson,

It's me! I'm pretty sure mail interception isn't much of a thing anymore, but if it is . . . well, sorry. I know you're both worried sick about me, so I decided I had to put you out of your misery. As you may have been able to tell from the stamp, I'm living the high life in a little place called Stockholm, and I've eaten so many meatballs that the police wouldn't be able to recognize me if they tried. I doubt I'll ever leave. Come winter I might be singing a different tune, but hey. Ingen ko på isen, *as the Swedes say.*

I have to say, Watermelonie, I do enjoy your new

name. I hear you're Lou-Lou's tour partner now? Very cute. Don't forget, if you neglect to invite me to your wedding, I'll never forgive you :)

On a more serious note, everyone else in our old playgroup seems to have vanished entirely off the map. I'm taking it as a good thing, but if you have any news, tell me.

Well, my hand is cramping, so that's all you get for now. There's a return address on the inside of the envelope.

With indifference,

The God of Beginnings

P.S. That's Janus, Lou-Lou.